LAST ONE TO DIE

ALSO BY CYNTHIA MURPHY

Win Lose Kill Die

CYNTHIA MURPHY

LAST

ONE

TO

DIE

DELACORTE PRESS

Text copyright © 2021 by Cynthia Murphy
Cover art copyright © Getty Images

All rights reserved. Published in the United States by Delacorte Press, an imprint of Random House Children's Books, a division of Penguin Random House LLC, New York. Originally published in paperback by Scholastic UK, London, in 2021.

Delacorte Press is a registered trademark and the colophon is a trademark of Penguin Random House LLC.

GetUnderlined.com

Educators and librarians, for a variety of teaching tools, visit us at RHTeachersLibrarians.com

Library of Congress Cataloging-in-Publication Data is available upon request.
ISBN 978-0-593-70554-4 (tr. pbk.) — ISBN 978-0-593-70555-1 (ebook)

The text of this book is set in 12.25-point Bembo Book MT Std.
Interior design by Megan Shortt

Printed in the United States of America
1st Printing
First American Edition

For my parents,
who raised me;
and
for Luke,
who saved me

LONDON BOROUGH POLICE

Interview Transcript

CASE NUMBER: 36926
DATE: June 28
INTERVIEWING OFFICER: Detective Moran
TRANSCRIPT PREPARED BY: Officer Bowers
INCIDENT TYPE: GBH
ADDRESS OF OCCURRENCE: ~~Cannon Street~~
                            ~~City of London~~
VICTIM NAME: ~~Mary Stevens~~
DOB: ~~12.27.2003~~

DETECTIVE MORAN: (rustling noises) OK, Miss Stevens. For the purposes of this tape, can you describe the events that took place early the morning of June twenty-eighth?

MARY STEVENS: I . . . Well, yeah, sort of. It was dark (audible sobs) and . . . and . . . (audible sobbing)

DM: Take your time.

1

MS: (audible sobbing)

DM: Let's start from the beginning, shall we? You stated that you had just left a party, is that correct?

MS: Yes.

DM: Were you alone? No? Please note for the tape that Miss Stevens is shaking her head in a negative gesture.

MS: No, not at first. But (audible sigh) my boy-friend and I had a fight—

DM: A physical altercation?

MS: What?

DM: A physical fight.

MS: Oh, right. No, just an argument. But he walked off.

DM: He left you alone? At (papers rustling) two-thirty a.m.?

MS: (barely audible) Yes.

DM: Can you recall where?

MS: Yeah, it was near the Tate, you know, near Millennium Bridge? Where you can see St. Paul's? I was upset. He knows how creepy I think it is around there, especially at night.

DM: And is this where the altercation happened? Yes? Please note for the tape that Miss Stevens is nodding.

MS: (barely audible) Yes.

DM: Can you tell me what you saw?

MS: Not really. Like I said, it was dark. Sorry. (pause) I suppose I heard him first.

DM: Him?

MS: I think so.

DM: But you aren't certain.

MS: No, but why would a woman . . . (audible sobbing)

DM: We just have to be sure. Speculation can be harmful in a case like . . . this.

MS: Right. A case like this. (pause) Well, I heard them, the person. They crept up on me, but I heard clicking, right before . . . (audible sobbing)

DM: Before?

MS: Before they did this to me.

DM: Please note for the tape that Miss Stevens is indicating lacerations from her collarbone across to her right shoulder.

MS: It didn't hurt at first. It just felt hot, then wet. Then I realized it was blood. So much blood . . .

DM: I'm sorry. (audible rustling) The initial report states that you were injured with a knifelike object?

MS: Not a knife. (barely audible) It was his—the person's—nails. He ripped my necklace off with them.

DM: Miss Stevens, I'm not sure I understand what you're trying to tell me.

MS: Their nails. They were made from metal.

End of Interview

1

This is it. My new life. A fresh start, no boy worries—just me, the big city, and my future.

At least that's what I thought until two minutes ago. "I'm sorry, miss. There ain't no Neev listed here."

I try really hard not to bite this guy's head off and force my lips into a smile instead.

"It's Gaelic," I explain, for the seventeenth time since I got off the boat. "It's spelled N-I-A-M-H."

"Oh." The little man behind the desk of my new hall of residence narrows his eyes and scans his list again. I notice the name on his polished steel badge says *Derek*. "Oh, yeah, here you are. Weird spelling."

A series of almighty thumps interrupt him, and I turn to see a tall, pretty brunette. She's busy dragging a huge suitcase down the steps into the foyer, panting from the effort.

"Excuse me," she starts, before focusing big brown eyes on me. "Oh, sorry. I'll wait."

"No, it's fine." I gesture toward the desk. "Go ahead." I'm getting nowhere here. It must be important if she dragged that massive bag all the way downstairs again. A cursory glance around had shown that there wasn't an elevator in the place.

"Oh, thank you so much!" She drops the case at the foot of the stairs and approaches the desk. A small diamond twinkles in her nose and I can't take my eyes off it, it's so cool. No one at home has their nose pierced, well unless you count Carrie Duncan from up the road—who got drunk and stuck her mom's hoop earring through her nostril—which I do not.

"Yeah?" Derek's face is impassive as the girl twirls a loose curl around one finger. She has that effortless look of someone with money. Her dark hair is glossy and shot through with streaks of gold, and a silk camisole hangs delicately from one shoulder. I'll bet anything it's vintage. "It's my room, it's too high up," she begins. "I need to change."

Derek holds up a raised palm. "No more rooms," he barks. "Irish here got the last one."

Nice.

"But I haven't even checked in yet," I protest.

The girl whirls on me, grabbing my arm. "You haven't?"

"Er, no, I've just arrived." I look down at her hand on my arm. She's not letting go.

Awkward.

"What floor is she on?" The girl turns those brown, melting eyes on the self-proclaimed guardian of the rooms and he checks his ledger.

"Second."

She turns to me again. "That's perfect! How are you with heights?"

"Er . . ." I don't know, is the honest answer. Most of the houses in the little town I'm from are bungalows, and there isn't a high-rise between my house and the next-closest city, not that I've ever seen, anyway. I liked standing on the top deck of the boat coming over, though. "Fine, I guess."

"Oh my God, I love your accent!" she squeals, pumping my arm so enthusiastically I can't help but laugh. "Would you swap? Pretty please? I'm on the tenth floor and I am just terrified of heights. Terrified. I can't even stand on a chair to change a light bulb."

She's so . . . eloquent, I think is the right word. I've never met anyone this stylish or charming in real life before. Her voice seems to drip honey and diamonds, compared to my country twang.

"Yeah, sure, that's fine with me." I turn to the man. "Is that all right with you, Derek?"

"Doesn't bother me." He shrugs. "Give Irish your keys, then," he says to the girl.

"It's Niamh," I repeat through gritted teeth.

The girl holds out a small, worn plastic key ring, its corners chipped and scratched, two small silver keys dangling from it. Room 1012. Mine for the next six weeks. "Like Neve Campbell? That's so retro!"

"Er, sure," I reply, taking the keys from her and smiling.

Mental note—find out who Neve Campbell is.

"Here." Derek thumps another set of keys and a thick folder of paperwork on his desk. Room 215, the room I should have been in. "Sign your name there, missy, and fill the rest of this out for tomorrow." He hands me a chewed blue pen that I take gingerly, with great care not to touch the chewed end. I practice my signature (any excuse) and hand it back. He doesn't bother to change our room numbers on the paperwork, I notice. I guess it doesn't really matter.

"Thank you so much!" The girl scoops up her new keys and dances back over to her luggage before turning to me. "Where are my manners! I'm Sara." She smiles. "I'll take this upstairs and then come and help with your bags, if you want?"

"No need." I grab the folder before swinging my large backpack on. "I travel light."

I almost laugh at the look of shock on her face.

"That's all you have? Seriously?"

I nod, feeling my cheeks warm up. I didn't have much to pack, not much that I wanted to bring to London, anyway. I didn't think my farming boots would go down too well here.

"Good for you, like a capsule wardrobe," she huffs, lugging her case up each step with a loud thump and a sigh. Derek pointedly ignores her and opens his newspaper, so I run to grab the other end of it. "Thanks. Didn't realize how much I'd packed until I had to drag it up and down here."

Sweat breaks out on the skin beneath my backpack immediately. "Is there really no elevator?"

"Oh, yeah," she replies, though it sounds more like *yah*. "There is, but only where the rooms are. Once we're up this flight, we can take the easy route."

"Thank God." I choke the words out, trying to hide my rattling breath as we navigate the narrow stairwell. We heft the case up to the next landing and I think we're home free, but suddenly I lurch forward. The papers in the folder I'm holding go flying over the top of the suitcase. One of its wheels is caught in a piece of upturned carpet.

"Oh, no!" Sara drops to her knees, gathering up my course documents while I wrestle the case back onto the landing. I finally manage to tear it free, my hairline prickling with sweat, as Sara hands a haphazard pile of papers out to me. "Here," she says, smiling. "Think I got it all."

"Thanks." Sara still manages to look impeccable as she wheels her case along the drab corridor, not a hair out of place. I spot manicured toenails peeking out of her sandals, their rose-gold straps highlighting her lightly tanned skin. The pale green paint on the walls is chipped at shoulder and hip height, as though many bodies have rubbed along this hall. Layers of white and yellow show beneath, a pattern of the building's past.

At the end of the corridor is the elevator. Sara presses a button and the doors groan open, beckoning us in. "Don't judge," she says as we step inside. "I know it's only one more floor, but I cannot face carrying this up another step."

"Same," I laugh, dropping the weight from my shoulders

and dragging myself into the elevator after her. The doors don't close immediately, so I perch precariously on my bag and try to shove my papers into some sort of order while Sara presses the buttons. A beautiful diamond cluster ring sparkles on her forefinger. God, she's effortlessly cool—that perfect mix of polished and casual chic. I wonder if I should put a couple of strategic rips into my jeans too.

"So," she says. "Which summer course are you taking?"

"Drama." I don't even try to keep the excitement out of my voice. I've worked my behind off all year saving for these six weeks and I can't believe I'm finally here.

"Hey, me too!" The doors shudder closed, and the elevator begins its jerky ascent. Before we can carry on the conversation, it wobbles to a stop and the doors open again for the second floor. Sara turns to me. "I guess this is me. Thanks again for swapping; I owe you. I would have died if I had to live on the tenth floor, seriously."

"No problem," I reply, embarrassed. "I'm just glad I'm here."

"Me too." She hesitates for a second, leaning on the doors so they don't close. "Hey, do you want to walk to class together in the morning? I don't know anyone else yet."

"I'd love to." Then I blurt out, "I don't know a soul here, either."

"Great!" She smiles, letting go of the doors. "Do you want to knock for me around eight-thirty? We can grab a coffee before we walk to the welcome event."

"Sure." I wave through the closing gap. I wonder if I can train myself overnight to like coffee. "See you in the morning."

I smile at my blurred reflection as the elevator lumbers up to my temporary new home. See, Niamh, you've already made a friend. You'll be great here.

The doors creak open and I'm faced with a corridor that is a carbon copy of the one downstairs: faded, with a subtle air of neglect. I grab the top handle of my bag, not able to pick it up again. I follow the numbers along the hall until I arrive at 1012. The key slots in easily.

I turn the handle, but the door is heavy, and I have to lean my weight against it before it opens. I enter a small, sparse room with nothing but a naked single bed, a desk, and a wardrobe that's seen better days.

Oh, and there's a window. Bonus.

I ditch my bag and let the door close softly as I run to press my face up against the glass, like an excited kid. The city glitters before me and I can pick out huge, up-lit buildings, though I'm not sure what they are. I scan the horizon with excitement—how big *is* this place? I spot the Thames snaking along beneath my window and my arms explode into goose bumps. You did it, girl, I think. All that hard work, all the mucking out horses and dirty farm jobs were totally worth it. You're here, you're finally here.

Despite my excitement, I'm absolutely shattered. It's been a long day of traveling and I want to be fresh for the morning. I open my bag and upend it on the desk, where a mini survival kit of Irish tea bags and chocolate bars topple out. God bless my sister. The rest of my meager belongings spill everywhere but I don't care. I'm too tired and I have no mom to tell me off for it.

Ohhh, no. Mom. I dig around for my phone, retrieving it from the backpack pocket I stashed it in earlier, and hunt for the charger. I plug it in and stare at the cracked screen, willing it to light up. Mom will kill me if I don't get in touch tonight.

To my relief, the screen blinks into life and I grab it, firing off a text to let her know I'm here safe, before switching it to silent. A few seconds later my phone bounces on the scarred wooden desk, but I ignore it. I can't deal with Mom tonight. I'll get up a little earlier tomorrow and call her then instead. Right now, I need to sleep. Grabbing pajamas and a hair tie, I eye the bare pillows and duvet, wondering how many bodies have slept in them before me. Am I too tired to care?

Yep, I think I am.

I change quickly, grab the pile of papers, and sit back on the bed, pressing my back to the cool, bare wall. I spread them out, digging around for tomorrow's schedule. Then I realize I have two of everything. Sara must have mixed hers up with mine.

I look down at my fleecy PJs, with tiny, fluffy sheep jumping lazily over fences decorating my legs.

I can't go downstairs in these.

I start to sort through the papers, making two piles—one for me and one for Sara. I can't believe the amount of stuff there is to fill in. Medical forms, housing stuff . . . Guilt gnaws at me. I should really take them down to Sara so she can get started on them. I stare at the jolly little sheep and sigh.

Sometimes I really am too nice.

I press the button for the elevator, scuffing my slippers along the tattered green carpet. The doors creak open and I get in. The elevator grinds to a halt on the second floor and a little bubble erupts in my stomach. What if Sara's asleep already? Have I totally misjudged this? I tug at the hem of my button-down top and slowly approach my could-have-been room. I hesitate for a second and knock.

No answer.

"Hey." A male voice makes me jump. "I don't think anyone's in there."

"Oh." I turn, but the figure is disappearing round the corner. I hesitate, then knock again, just in case. "Sara?"

Nothing.

Something makes me try the handle. To my surprise, the door opens easily.

"Sara?" I call into the room. Silence.

She must be out, then. I'll just leave the papers on her desk, no harm done.

It's dark in Sara's room, with the curtains pulled tightly shut. I guess she really is scared of heights, even on the second floor.

The smell hits me suddenly, something raw and primal that turns my stomach. I inch farther into the room on autopilot, even though my brain is screaming at me to get out. Something is not right. My eyes adjust to the darkness. In the gloom I can just about decipher the bed, and a huddled figure lying on it, one arm hanging limply over the edge.

The door is ajar and as I step forward, a slice of light from the hall lands on the bed. I see eyes wide and staring. Clumps of hair scattered across the pillow, ripped from the roots. A long, slim hand trailing toward the carpet, a beautiful diamond cluster ring on its forefinger.

A forefinger that is steadily dripping with blood, forming a dark pool on the floor.

2

"You all right, Irish?"

Derek plonks a steaming mug down on the table in front of me. I try to nod. His voice is kind, but I'm completely numb.

"Best thing after a shock, tea with sugar." I am silent, staring at the chipped rim, and Derek walks away, still rattling off the benefits of a sugary brew. I can't get Sara's face out of my head. I've seen dead bodies before—at home there was a wake every other month and they always have an open casket—but they always seemed unreal. Plastic.

Sara's body was still warm when I found her.

"Excuse me, miss . . ."

I refocus my eyes to see a young guard. Police officer, I remind myself.

"Hughes," I supply, as he checks his notepad.

"Miss Hughes," he repeats. "I'm Officer Bowers. I need to ask you a few more questions, if you feel up to it?"

I nod. Not that there's much I can tell him. I ran from the room screaming as soon as I saw Sara's body and refused to return.

"You said earlier that you swapped rooms with the deceased, is that correct?"

"Yes." My voice sounds rusty. "She said she didn't like heights. And my room was on the second floor, so . . ." I choke on the words.

"And you had never met before?"

"No."

"So why did you swap rooms?"

I open my mouth to explain, but Derek materializes in front of me. "She a suspect?"

"Excuse me?" The officer looks pretty pissed off at the interruption.

"Miss Hughes here, she a suspect?"

"These are routine questions, sir."

"I don't mind . . ." I start, but Derek, to my immense surprise, cuts me off.

"Don't say anything else," he warns me, before turning back to the officer. "She ain't answering nothing without a lawyer present, all right?"

The officer flushes. "They're really just routine, sir." He squirms a little and I realize Derek is right. I'm a suspect.

"Routine, my eye," says Derek. "You wanna question her, then take her down to the station and give her a lawyer. Otherwise, leave her be. Poor girl's had a massive shock, and she's a minor too." The officer consults his notes and frowns.

"That not in your notes? She's sixteen and I'm in loco parentis for the present moment. Everything goes through me, right? No need to worry her parents with this yet." He puffs his chest out. "You'll need my permission to question her any further."

I think my eyes are in danger of falling out of my head.

"Is this true?" The officer directs the question at me, though I can tell Derek has rattled him. I nod, not really understanding half of what's going on. Derek, the dark horse. "Fine," says the officer. "We'll be in touch."

He marches out of the foyer and I gawk at Derek. He winks at me.

"Close your mouth and drink your tea, Irish, or you'll be catching flies."

"Mammy, I'm fine, honestly." I hold the pay phone slightly away from my ear and gaze dully out the dirt-streaked window as she rants about the dangers of the Big City and threatens to get on the next flight over. Derek's done his best to be reassuring; he didn't tell her too much, especially about me finding Sara, but he underestimated the neurosis of the average Irish mother.

"Niamh, I want you home. One night away and someone has died. Been killed, no less. Holy Mother of God, we're lucky it wasn't you, girl."

"I know," I mutter. I've been trying not to think about it. "But I want to stay. If anything, it's safer now. They've moved us to a different dorm. There's a guard on patrol."

"No way, absolutely not . . ."

I hold the phone away again and study the graffiti that decorates the phone booth. It stinks in here. How did people use these before cell phones? They're claustrophobic and disgusting. But the charge on my phone didn't last two minutes this morning. I push the door ajar with my foot and search for my hand sanitizer with my free hand.

"Mom," I interrupt as the phone beeps a warning, "my time's about to run out. I'm staying. I've worked too hard to give up before I even start."

"Niamh . . ."

"Please?"

She huffs down the phone and I know I've won, for the moment.

"Fine, but I'm telling you now, girl, if it wasn't for Granny H being ill again . . ."

"I know. How is she?"

She sighs. "The same. She didn't recognize your daddy the other day."

"Oh, Mom. I miss her."

"I'm sorry, love. I know you do. Listen, now. You will get your cell fixed immediately and call home every day. I'll get your daddy to transfer the money for repairs right now, OK?"

"OK."

"I mean it. Every single day, Niamh Marie. And get in touch with your sister once in a while, would you? She's driving us all crazy, climbing the walls without you. Promise?"

"I promise." It's a small price to pay for being allowed to stay. Although the thought of going home to our safe little town is very tempting right now. I miss them. I'm not going to let her know that, though.

"I love you, Niamh."

"Love you too. Say hi to Daddy for me and tell Meghan I'll send some pictures later."

"Bye, love——" She's cut off as my money finally runs out.

"Bye," I whisper into the handset before setting it back in its cradle. I stare at the silent phone. Am I doing the right thing? Should I be staying here at all? I liberally coat my hands in sanitizer and rub it in, wishing it worked on memories too.

A loud tap on the glass makes my skin shrink on my bones.

"You done?" A tall, scruffy guy is glaring at me through the window, eyes sharp between long, greasy strands of hair.

"Yeah, sure." I push the door open. "All yours." He grunts and pushes past me. Honestly, city people. So rude. "You're welcome," I mutter, hoisting my bag onto my shoulder and crossing the quiet road, my damp hands tingling in the morning breeze.

There it is. The London Academy of Dramatic Arts rears up in front of me, a gray concrete building that manages to look both imposing and dated. It feels silly to be taking a drama course after what happened the past twelve hours. Frivolous, almost. I tell myself it's what Sara would have wanted.

Well, I'm pretty sure it is. It's definitely what Granny H would have wanted, if she remembered who I was. She was the actress of the family, back in her heyday, a semi-famous soap starlet. One of us has to carry on the tradition.

Right?

"Walk! You, yes, you—walk! Walk to a space with PUR-POSE! Walk like you really MEAN IT! Walk like you have SOMEWHERE TO GO!"

Oh, Lord. I've made a terrible mistake.

I furrow my brow and march to the other side of the room. Was I going to be doing this for the next six weeks? Walking? When I landed a spot in one of the country's most prestigious acting courses, trudging around a drab studio was not what I had in mind. Where was the stage? The dressing rooms? A script?

Anything but walking.

"Stop," bellows Miss Joanne, the instructor. Her voice belies her size; she's tiny and was evidently a dancer at some point. Her feet are perpetually turned out and her hair is slicked back into an immaculate bun. "Find a space in the room. Now. Make yourself as small as possible, a tiny seed in the earth."

I peek at the others in the room. Twenty kids, all curling their bodies into the fetal position. I make sure my backside is facing the wall so I don't moon anyone on the first day. Honestly, what possessed me to put a T-shirt dress on for a workshop? I'll stick to leggings from now on.

"Now grow! Become tall, stretch, raise those arms, like branches toward the sun. . . ."

I glance around again, watching arms flail and faces earnestly turn to the ceiling.

I thought the walking was bad.

I endure the rest of the class, which seems to last forever, including some excruciating "icebreakers." (Seriously, does anyone ever enjoy those things? Painful.) I'm grateful when lunch is called; I haven't eaten a full meal since I arrived.

The upside is that at least the morning activities kept me busy. Now I can't stop thinking about Sara, how she should be here, how we should be rolling our eyes about that class together. Her eyes. Sara's wide, staring eyes sear into my eyelids every time I blink. I shake my head. Stop it. Try to move on.

I follow the crowd to the small cafeteria on campus, but the food is expensive, which I didn't think about. I should at least have a drink, though, so I grab a Coke, Derek's advice about sugar being good for shock echoing in my ears. He was great last night, a welcome surprise. I hope he's stationed at the new dorms too.

Little pockets of people have already formed at the tables, and I try desperately to look like I know what I'm doing. I'm about to escape to the bathroom so I don't have to sit alone when a girl, a petite blond sitting at one of the tables, waves me over. Jasmine, I think her name is.

"Hi!" She pats the space next to her. "It's Niamh, right? Come and sit down."

I grin at her in relief and nod, sliding onto the edge of the bench. There are two guys and another girl from class at the

21

table. The guys nod in greeting. The girl smiles at me, then drops her head, studying the label on her food intently.

"I love your accent," Jasmine says, putting a tiny hand on my arm. I think of Sara, and a lump forms in my throat. "My great-grandma was Irish, you know." I nod politely. Wasn't everyone's?

"Thanks," I murmur, wishing I'd just legged it to the girls' room. I feel huge next to Jasmine, she's so teeny. I eye the festival wristbands that decorate both wrists and idly wonder how old she is. I wasn't allowed to go to a music festival until I was eighteen—unless you counted the Kilkenny music festival, which I did not. "Cool wristbands."

"Oh, thanks. They're from last summer." She takes a sip out of her reusable water bottle. "It was pretty epic."

I nod, unsure of what to say next, and so I follow her lead and take a sip of my Coke.

"So, Niamh, tell us." Her voice drops to a stage whisper and her eyes dart around the table, as though she's checking for an audience. "Is it true?"

"Is what true?" I ask, confused.

"You know," she whispers, leaning so close I can smell her citrusy-fresh shampoo. I realize the rest of the table have gone quiet and are watching me too. "That you found a body."

I freeze. Is she serious?

"Jas, stop," the label girl across from me warns, but Jasmine presses on regardless.

"We heard about it this morning." Her voice is full of

gleeful curiosity. "Is it true? Did you really find a dead girl in the dorms? Is that why we've all been moved?"

"Yeah," I say. And immediately regret it.

"No way!" Jasmine practically explodes from her chair. She grasps my forearms and my heart thumps, like an animal who has to gnaw off their own limb to escape danger. "You're lying."

"Jasmine!" The other girl puts down the food wrapper and shakes her head. "Stop it."

"Chill, Tasha." Jasmine glares at the girl across from me and resumes her inquisition. "Everyone's saying she was murdered. Is it true? Did you see anything?" Her eyes grow wide and she pulls away slightly. "Oh my god. Are you a suspect?"

My vision blurs. Oh, no. Not here. I cannot cry here.

I mutter something about having to go and push myself up from the bench. The table screeches and I hear the thump of my open Coke bottle fall behind me, but there's no way I'm turning back. I stubbornly wipe the tears from my eyes and run to the nearest bathroom, where I lock myself in a stall and sit down heavily on the toilet lid.

This has to be the worst first day in the history of first days. Ever.

My sobs eventually slow down, turning into gentle hiccups until I lean back against the wall and set off the automatic flush, which of course makes me jump and sets off another flood of tears. Maybe I should listen to my mother after all. Call it quits.

I peel a wad of tissues from the dispenser and dab at my face, though why I'm attempting to save my makeup I have no idea. I take a deep, shaky breath, stand up on wobbly legs, and open the door, stopping in surprise when I see a figure at the sinks. I didn't hear anyone come in. The girl's face is obscured by a long, shiny curtain of dark hair, but then she looks up and I recognize her as Jasmine's friend. Tasha.

She's currently dabbing at a brown stain on her white top. The spilled Coke.

"Oh, hey." Tasha catches my eye in the mirror. "You OK? You left in kind of a hurry."

I gesture at her top. "I'm sorry, I didn't mean to . . ."

"Hey, don't worry. I'm just sorry you didn't get Jasmine too." She smiles, her eyes full of sympathy. "She was kind of awful back there."

"Yeah." I wash my hands slowly, rubbing the foamy soap carefully over each finger, seeing glimpses of Sara's bloody hand as I do.

"So it is true, then," Tasha whispers. "Sorry," she adds quickly. "I'm being as bad as Jas. You don't have to talk about it."

I sigh. Is this what happens if I stay? I'm the girl who found a body?

"It's OK," I say. Might as well set the story straight. I meet her eyes in the mirror as I yank paper towels from the dispenser. "Yeah, it's true. Her name was Sara. I only met her last night, and then . . ." The words stick in my throat and I lean against the wall.

"And then she was dead?" Tasha whispers. I nod and another hot trail trickles down my cheek.

And then she was dead.

"I'm so sorry."

"Yeah." What else do I say? "I didn't know her, really, but she seemed nice."

Tasha shakes her head. "No one deserves that. Are they sure it wasn't . . . you know . . ."

"What, suicide? No." I swallow. There's silence for a moment.

"I really am sorry about soaking you," I say. "Here." I rummage in my shoulder bag and pull a crumpled black cardigan from the bottom. It's dotted with tiny, sparkling buttons and has matching little cuffs on the elbow length sleeves. I haven't even worn it yet and it cost a small fortune—it was my I'm-off-to-live-in-London cardigan. "It's clean, just a bit wrinkled. You can borrow it if you want. It should fit."

"Are you sure?"

"Of course, take it."

Tasha grins and disappears into a stall, reemerging with her damp top wadded in her hands. She shoves it into a pocket of her bag and straightens up, admiring her reflection.

"This is so pretty!" She brushes her fingers along the velvet ribbon that lines the closure. "I'll give it back to you tomorrow, pinkie promise."

"It looks good on you." I offer a watery smile. Tasha nods toward the door. "Are you coming?" I hesitate.

"I mean, I'll walk with you," Tasha offers, before adopting a dramatic pose, "but only if you do it with *purpose*."

I grin and follow her out the door. Maybe this won't be so bad after all.

3

The afternoon is much more bearable. No more workshops, we're told, just a lecture about what we'll be doing for the next few weeks.

As we file into the lecture hall and wait for the speakers, Tasha and I chat. I warm to her immediately. She's from a little town up in the North of England and we quickly bond over the desperation to leave our hometowns for somewhere more exciting. I knew I wasn't the only one.

The room is warm, and the lights have been dimmed. Past students are projected on a big screen in the front, sharing their experiences of being on work placements out in the wider community. Work placements are a requirement of the program—I've never completed one before, but I'm excited to try out a real job, even if I'm not being paid for it. I try my best to listen to a redhead discussing the challenges of pretending to be an animal for the tourists at the zoo. Good God, please don't let that be my work placement. We'll receive our assignments in the next few days.

"Hey." Tasha nudges me and I realize I'm close to dozing off. She hands me her phone. "Put in your number there." I pull my phone out of my bag and show her the cracked screen. She grimaces.

"I need to get it fixed after class so I can call home," I whisper. "My mother is having a fit."

"Can't think why," Tasha replies. "You only discovered a murder."

I start to reply, when we're shushed by the girl in front. We promptly dissolve into silent giggles and return our attention to the proud graduate who is now sharing the life lessons she learned while pretending to be a tiger.

Once I've waved goodbye to Tasha, I walk to the nearby phone repair shop that she Googled for me. It's just around the corner. They promise to have it fixed before they close, but that's more than three hours away, so I decide to go back to the cafeteria and finally read the course material while I wait.

I head to the cafeteria but spy Jasmine holding court with a group at the little coffee bar in the corner, all holding refillable coffee cups and loudly discussing the lack of "real" vegan options on the menu. I swerve down the nearest corridor before she can spot me and force me to relive the worst moment of my life, and land in front of a pair of double doors bearing a small plaque that reads LIBRARY.

Perfect.

I push open one of the large wooden doors and pass through the gray security gates that stand on either side. It's dark and a little cramped in here, but I immediately feel safe, cocooned. I love libraries.

I wander past the checkout desk to my left and inch forward to trail my fingers over the large, leather padded table in the center of the room. It's encircled by rickety wooden chairs, and tall shelves loom above me on a second level, a short flight of steps leading up into the stacks, which stand tall behind a wooden railing. I'm staring up into the gloom, marveling at the height of the shelves, all those books, when a tall, lanky figure emerges from them and sends my pulse racing.

"Oh!" I hold a hand up to my chest, a thump sounding loudly behind my breastbone. It's the guy from the phone booth earlier, and he looks just as unfriendly, glaring at me with the same cutting stare. His hair is stringy in the overhead lights and startlingly dark against his pale, waxy skin. His mouth and chin are peppered with painful-looking acne. "Sorry, I didn't know there was anyone else here."

He says nothing, just grabs a trolley, grunts, and disappears back into the darkness. The wheels squeak behind him.

"Don't mind him." Another small heart attack rocks me as a friendly voice pipes up from behind. I spin around to see a small, plump woman emerge from a little office behind the checkout desk. "That's just Will, the library assistant. He doesn't talk much." She smiles and I immediately warm to her; there's something comforting and motherly about her. "Can I help you?"

"I was just looking for somewhere quiet." My voice is croaky. I clear my throat and hold up my enrollment folder. "To read this. Is that OK?"

"Of course!" She walks around the desk and I see she's leaning on a cane and breathing heavily. "We don't get many people in here in the summer months. I can give you a temporary library card, if you'd like?"

"That would be great." I agree, and she shuffles back to her computer, fingers flying deftly over the keys.

"Which course are you taking?"

"Drama."

"How wonderful. And you came all the way from Ireland?"

"Yes." I rattle off my information and she fills it in, chattering constantly.

"Brave girl." She smiles. "Now, look at the camera annnnnd say 'cheese'!"

I force a semblance of a smile and the webcam clicks.

"Lovely." She hums a little tune while the computer prints my ID card and then she hands it over. It's still warm. "Now you can borrow anything you'd like. Apart from the Special Collections, that is."

"Special Collections?"

"Yes, the really rare stuff." Her eyes twinkle behind silver-rimmed glasses. "We have some pages from an original Shakespeare folio and other bits and pieces you might be interested in, especially if you're thinking of applying for the scholarship."

My ears prick up.

"Scholarship? Oh, I'm only in the summer program, I don't think I could . . ."

"Oh, you certainly could." The librarian riffles through a pile of leaflets and extracts one before handing it over to me. "There are a few, but here is a specific one I think you'd be interested in. You can win a place to study drama here and receive credits toward your final year. It should all be in your enrollment packet there. I think the deadline is fairly soon, though."

"Wow, thank you." I feel a flutter of excitement despite the horrific start to my day. "I haven't had a chance to read it yet, but I'll definitely take a look."

She winks at me. "Make sure you do. Now, make yourself at home. We don't close until eight, so you have plenty of time."

"Thank you, er . . ."

"Ruth."

"OK, thanks, Ruth."

I settle at the large table and spread the course material in front of me, realizing I still have two of everything. I push the copies to the side, then pick up the scholarship brochure and try my best to focus, to concentrate on what I'm reading. The full-time course looks wonderful, nothing like the workshops this morning. Real acting, time in the theater, learning about its history. I glance at the requirements and see that part of it is an essay, some kind of research into London's theatrical history. It sounds pretty cool. I try to keep reading but I'm exhausted, last night's lack of sleep finally catching up with me. The words start to blur, my eyelids heavy, and when I feel someone gently shaking my shoulder, I realize I must have dozed off.

"Sorry to wake you, but we're closing soon." My brain takes a second to catch up and I look at my watch. Ten to eight. I sit up in panic.

"My phone!" I blurt, jumping out of my chair. "Thanks a million, Ruth. Sorry for nodding off."

She waves the comment away.

"Just don't broadcast how cozy we are for a nap; we'll be overrun. See you soon, I hope."

"For sure." I run to the door and bolt down to the phone shop, where the owner is just about to pull the shutters. I manage to convince him to let me in, and in minutes my new, crack-free screen is in my hands.

I call home as I walk back to the new dorms. I did promise, after all.

I get to class early the next morning, hoping to catch Tasha before workshops start. I spot a gaggle of people I vaguely recognize from yesterday gathered by one of the lecture halls and wander over. They are crowded around a list pinned on the wall.

Of course—our work placements. Each of us has to go

out and use our acting skills in the community. We heard about some awful-sounding ones yesterday, but there were also some pretty cool ones, like working with vulnerable kids at council-funded drama camps. I was hoping for something like that, though knowing my luck, I'd be spending two days a week at the zoo, peeling bananas with my feet.

Keeping my eye out for Tasha, I wander over and wait my turn as the crowd thins a little. I finally get to the front and squint down the list, picking my name out. I'm going to be placed somewhere called the Victorian Street Museum. Hmmm. Not quite what I was hoping for, but it doesn't sound as bad as the zoo. I look for Jasmine's name and pray that one is all hers but no such luck—she, of course, got the one I was hoping for. Typical. I scan the list for Tasha too, hoping we might be placed together, but I don't see her name anywhere. There are two long black marker lines drawn across the pages. One must be covering Sara's name. She'd never get to do her placement now.

"Look who it is." A familiar smell invades my nostrils: lemons and soap. I turn around to see Jasmine's small frame pushing through the crowd. "The gypsy."

"What are you on about now?" The nerve of this girl. I've had enough of her already; she's clearly toxic.

"You put a curse on anyone who tries to be your friend. Isn't that right, gypsy?"

I push away from her and head toward the library. I'm not getting caught up in her racist little attack.

"Yeah, you should leave. Where are you going? Off

to play with your voodoo dolls? You're not welcome here, Niamh. You've caused enough trouble."

That's enough. She doesn't even have her insults right. I whirl on her, anger bubbling under my skin. "What exactly are you talking about, Jasmine?"

"Oh." Her eyes widen with smug glee. "You really haven't heard."

"Heard what?"

"About Tasha." My blood rapidly cools, forming ice in my veins.

"What about her?"

"She was attacked." She spits the words out almost joyfully, her eyes sparkling with vindictive pleasure.

Nonononono. She's lying. She has to be.

"Last night on her way home. She's in a coma. The doctors don't know if she'll survive another night." Jasmine steps close and I wince as she pushes her sharp fingers into my shoulder. "That's two girls who've been nice to you ending up hurt or dead," she hisses, spit flecking into my face. "*I* won't be making the same mistake."

I stand there, numb, as she turns on her heel and walks away.

4

I spend lunchtime in the bathroom. Despite my prime eaves-
dropping position in the end stall, I don't get any actual details
on how Tasha is doing. I'm too nervous to ask anyone. People
have avoided me all morning. Jasmine has done a good job of
spreading her poison.

Poor Tasha. I wish I could visit her or something. I wonder if I can find out which hospital she's at. Maybe Derek
could help.

I finally emerge from the stall when it falls quiet outside
and I creak the door open, praying everyone will already be
in afternoon class. I debate signing myself out sick but decide
to just skip it and visit my museum placement a little earlier
instead. I'm not really supposed to be there until later this
week, but I need a change of scenery and hopefully no one
will even notice I'm gone. On my way out, I double-check
the list. I'm the only student going to the museum, which is

good. Two days a week away from the accusatory glances and Jasmine's nasty comments will be a welcome relief.

I map the route on my phone and see that the museum is a few stops away on the train—either that or a forty-minute walk. I hesitate. I haven't tackled the Underground yet and if I'm honest, its mess of swirling-colored lines terrifies me. The walk seems decent, though, and grateful I donned my Nikes this morning, I plug my earphones in and get going.

I let myself be distracted by the sights, so I'm in my own little world when the riverbank sneaks up on me. Millennium Bridge rises out of the Thames, its narrow expanse rammed with tourists.

I wander to the middle, wondering if I'm imagining the bounce of the bridge, and angle my phone so I can snap a photo of Tower Bridge. I send the picture to my sister.

It's a warm, balmy day and I turn my face up to the sun, letting the horror of the last couple of days drift away. I pause, trying to get my bearings, and spot the Shard glittering in the distance, a tall, fierce building that punctures the skyline. The museum is somewhere off in that direction, tucked down a side street, from what I could gather on its website. I peel myself away, my eyes lingering on Shakespeare's Globe as I pass it by. Wow. A sign shows there are groundling tickets for a play on sale, which would mean standing through the whole performance, but they're cheap and I decide to make sure I come back this way later.

I'm really here. This is the city I always imagined visiting one day, the place I saved all that money for. And now I'm here. I can hardly believe it.

The area hums with energy. I pass bars and restaurants, crowds of people spilling out onto the pavements and perching on the riverbank walls.

I stop to check the route and see that Meghan has replied to the Tower Bridge photo.

When can I come?! Miss you xo

I tap a note back, telling her to work on Mom and Daddy to let her come over for a week at the end of my course. Wishful thinking on my part, I know, but she was gutted when I left.

The crowds disappear swiftly once I venture into the streets behind the South Bank. It's a bit more industrial here and I can see the history etched into the walls. I walk past old redbrick buildings that once housed mills and factories. I follow the map beneath an old railway arch and down a cobbled street, before a robotic voice abruptly announces my arrival. Sure enough, two frosted glass doors, emblazoned with the museum logo, slide open and a cool, welcome blast of air-conditioning greets me. I descend the stairs beyond them.

"Welcome to the Victorian Street Museum," a middle-aged man in a topcoat and tails and a top hat booms from behind the counter in front of me. "How may I assist in your visit today?"

"Oh, hi. I'm here for my drama school placement."

He hikes up a pair of bushy salt-and-pepper brows and consults the wrought iron clock on the brick wall.

"Ah, yes. You're early, my dear! You must be eager! It's young Natasha, isn't it?"

My heart sinks. So we should have been placed together after all.

"No, sorry." I stumble over the words, my tongue thick in my throat. "I'm Niamh."

He consults something on the computer and his mouth gives an almost imperceptible twitch. "My mistake. I was told not to expect you."

"Oh. No, it's Tasha who won't be here."

"Of course, my apologies." He tips his head, so the brim of his hat casts hollow shadows over his eyes, and I shiver. I tell myself it's just the air-conditioning. He leans closer and flashes a toothy smile. "A terrible state of affairs, isn't it? You know . . ." He looks around and lowers his voice conspiratorially. "I heard it's not the first attack this week, either. Did you know a young woman died?"

My face must clearly say that, yes, I do know. I blink back tears as he looks at me blankly.

"Well." He claps his hands together with forced cheeriness. "Let me call someone to man the desk and I'll take you on the grand tour. Make yourself comfortable."

"Thank you," I murmur.

I wander to the brochure rack by the entrance and half-heartedly study the glossy leaflets, more to distract myself than anything. I pick up one for the museum itself. It's featured on a local ghost tour, which Meghan would love, but the idea turns my stomach a little now.

The last thing I need to see is a ghost.

"Ready, miss?" The man reappears, followed by a small, curly-haired woman in a bonnet who replaces him behind the desk. "Sue, this is young Niamh, our new Jane!" She greets me curtly. Friendly soul.

"Ready?" the man says with a smile. "Let's go."

I follow my tour guide through the turnstile and into the museum. "I'm Geoffrey." He smiles beneath his heavy white beard, extending a large, warm hand, which swallows my hesitant one. "I'm the performance coordinator here at the museum. Any problems, please come to me. I'll show you around and give you a bit of history before outlining your duties. How does that sound?"

"Great, thank you," I reply. His demeanor has totally changed, and I wonder if I imagined the sinister edge to him. I mean, he's more Santa than Satan now. I follow him through a small gift shop ("The tours begin and end here—clever marketing, don't you think?") and down a short, dark corridor.

The scene at the other end of it takes my breath away.

Victorian shopfronts line a cobbled street, and for a second I think we've gone back outside. Bright sunlight streams in from behind old, lead-lined windows, and I have to remind myself that we are definitely below street level. A mixture of odors fill the air: hot cocoa, tobacco smoke, and something farmyard-familiar and slightly unpleasant. It's like stepping onto the set of a period drama.

"It's quite something, isn't it?" Geoffrey's voice still manages to boom even though he's barely speaking above a whisper. I nod, speechless. "This building was once a cotton mill. The upstairs section was converted into overpriced apartments long ago, but when the contractors who bought it looked at the deeds, they realized this was all down here. That was when it was decided to preserve it as a museum."

"How did it all get here?"

"The great-grandson of the original mill owner was quite the wealthy eccentric. He was a doctor who enjoyed collecting bits and pieces of local history. He purchased shops and businesses that were about to be torn down back at the turn of the century. Then he had them all reassembled here, beneath the old mill. A kind of large-scale cabinet of curiosities, I suppose." I gaze around in awe, imagining all the work that must have gone into this place. "Of course"—Geoffrey lowers his rumbling voice—"there are accounts of the place being terribly haunted, but that's a story for another time. Can't say I've ever seen anything myself, mind. Ah." He straightens up suddenly, making me jump as he taps his silver-tipped cane and points it toward a figure emerging from the gloom. "Tommy! Come over here and meet our latest victim—I mean *recruit*." He laughs heartily, and I try to join in, but my mouth is full of sawdust. "Niamh, Tommy; Tommy, Niamh."

"Pleasure to meet you, miss," he says jokingly, and sweeps his flatcap off to tip it in my direction before I can get a good look at his face. Like Geoffrey, he's dressed in period costume, but while my guide is obviously a higher-class sort, Tommy has something of a street-urchin vibe about him. I try to get a good look as he replaces the hat and realize that the entire room has gone dark except for the glow from a tall black streetlamp.

"You too," I say, distracted. "Is there something wrong with the lights, Geoffrey?"

"Oh, no." Tommy smiles. His teeth flash white in the dark and I spy the shadow of a dimple in his left cheek. I'm a sucker for dimples. "They're on a timer. It's rigged so it goes from sunrise to sunset every fifteen minutes. Listen." Sure enough, I hear the faint hoot of an owl, where I'm fairly certain there was birdsong not long ago. "It's all to add to the atmosphere." It gradually becomes a little lighter. The dark blond strands of hair that peek from his cap gleam in the gathering light. He is *gorgeous*.

"Tommy here is a volunteer too." Geoffrey's voice breaks the spell—I almost forgot he was here. "Feel free to ask him anything."

Tommy beams at me and hooks his thumbs behind the suspenders holding up his loose cotton trousers. "Absolutely anything." He grins. I'm grateful it's not fully light in here. Oh, my.

"Come on, let me show you the staff area and find your costume, Niamh." Tommy gives me a mischievous wave as I follow Geoffrey once more, desperately trying not to trip over my own feet. My knees have turned to jelly, and my cheeks are flaming. I chance one more look behind me, but he's already gone. My heart drops somewhere around my knees.

Oh, girl. You're in trouble.

41

I twirl around in the small staff dressing room, admiring myself in the mirror. I thought I'd end up with some kind of tacky Victorian maid's outfit, but instead I'm wearing one of the most beautiful dresses I've ever seen.

It turns out I'll be playing the part of the wealthy mill owner's daughter, loosely based on the family who once lived here. It'll be my job to wander around the street with my little wicker basket, approaching groups who visit to tell them stories, all the while taking on the persona of an early-nineteenth-century lady. I have a bit of recommended reading to do from Geoffrey, to get myself caught up with the history of the area. I think of Ruth at the library. I'm pretty sure she'll be able to help me out.

I dig my phone out of my newly allocated locker. Meghan definitely needs to see this dress; she'll lose her mind over it. Luckily, as it's only a costume, it doesn't have the layers of corsetry and petticoats that Geoffrey assured me were the order of the day, but some clever dressmaking has created the illusion of both.

I snap a mirror selfie, poking my tongue out for my sister's benefit, and study the picture before I send it. The fabric of the dress is a shiny, satiny silk, embroidered all over with tiny sprigs of pink blossom and delicate green leaves. It has a high, square neckline, overlaid with the most delicate lace. Wide sleeves puff out from my shoulders before tightly gathering back in at the elbow, where they enclose my arms all the way down to the wrists. Tiny buttons march down the front of the bodice to my waist, which is wrapped in a thick black velvet ribbon. The skirt billows out in an explosion of fabric, skimming the floor and sweeping a large circle around my feet.

I feel like a princess.

I loosen my hair from its messy French braid and smile as the dark waves cascade down my back. Perfect. I send the first picture to Meghan and take another, of the back this time. The ribbon around my waist is thicker at the rear and a large bow sits atop the small bustle, which I adore. I pout and add a little crown emoji to the photo and send that one too, before I realize there's no signal on my phone, nothing at all. Great. Must be because we're in the basement—I bet the walls are two feet thick in an old building like this.

I shove my cell back in my locker and close the door. A few of them have already been claimed, some decorated with scraps of masking tape that have names scrawled across them, and others, like Geoffrey's, with more permanent, laminated signs. I don't see Tommy's name, though some of them have been left blank. I spot a roll of masking tape and a felt-tip pen on the shelf below the mirror. Perfect. I peel off a piece, rip the end and stick it on my locker, printing my name with a flourish. There. I am officially a member of the performance team.

I can't decide whether I'm more nervous or excited as I walk back to the museum floor and I marvel at where I am. Has it really been only two days? It feels like a lifetime ago since I waved goodbye to my family, but it was only Saturday night. Crazy.

"Niamh?" Tommy is holding court in the middle of a tour group as I enter. He looks up and his eyes lock on me. My skirt whispers along the floor, flirting with the cobblestones. His eyes on mine make me feel like the prettiest girl in the world. Well, they do until I realize I still have my neon pink sneakers on. I do my best to hide them, making a mental note to pack my ballet pumps for my actual shifts here.

"Hey," I reply, suddenly uncertain under his—and now the crowd's—avid gaze. Did I forget to zip up the dress or something? "What's wrong?" I twist my body around, craning my neck to check the back. All looks fine to me.

"Nothing," he breathes, his eyes narrowed and tight. He approaches me slowly, as though I'm a venomous snake he might have to subdue. "You look . . . different, that's all."

"Yeah," I joke, desperate to break the intensity. "Not quite my usual farm-girl getup, all right."

He just stares at me.

"I live on a farm, you know, at home?" He nods, his blue eyes not moving from mine. OK, then.

This is intense.

"Well, young Niamh." Oh, thank God. Geoffrey approaches and his booming voice breaks the silence. I turn gratefully toward it. "You look the part, I must say. A superb Jane."

"Jane?" Tommy echoes.

"Yes," Geoffrey says, bowing toward a couple of tourists who have broken away from Tommy's group and are strolling past. They smile at us before moving on. "Jane was the daughter of the mill owner here. Your dress is modeled on an old portrait that was found down here during the renovations." He looks at me closely. "I must say, the drama school did a wonderful job. The resemblance is quite uncanny, isn't it, Tommy?"

Tommy nods mutely—he still hasn't taken his eyes off me.

"Oh, well, that's good, isn't it?" My voice sounds uncertain even to me. There is something off here, and I don't know what.

"It is indeed!" Geoffrey is clearly delighted. "Come, she's hanging in the dressing room." He chuckles when he notices the blood drain from my face. "The portrait, my dear, Jane's portrait. You should see it. It really is quite uncanny."

I trail after him reluctantly. Tommy doesn't move and when I turn to check if he's following, he's melted back into the shadows, the automatic timers slowly returning the street to dusk.

Geoffrey pauses in front of me, holding a door ajar, and gestures for me to take the lead. I enter a Victorian lady's dressing room, complete with ornate dressing table, padded chair, and an oval looking glass.

Only, I realize, it's not a mirror. It's a portrait. An old portrait of a young, pale-skinned girl of around sixteen. A smattering of freckles dusts her nose, and dark, wavy hair tumbles over the lace collar at her throat. The embroidery on her dress seems to shimmer and large sleeves gather around her elbows.

I'm not actually looking in a mirror—but I might as well be.

5

"You're so overdramatic!" Meghan laughs at me from the screen. "She hardly looks like you."

"She does so," I reply, tracing my nails over the stone wall outside the museum. The air is warm, welcome after the air-conditioning inside. My induction is officially over, and my first full shift will be later this week. I was a bit freaked out about the portrait, so I called my darling sister, who immediately looked the damn thing up online and is still mocking me for it.

"Yeah, yeah." She scrambles back up the bed and into a sitting position. Our room is a dump.

"What have you been doing to the room? I've only been gone five minutes!"

Meghan shrugs. "Fashion show. I figured your wardrobe was fair game, what with you being away from home."

"What?" Another peal of laughter echoes from the tinny speakers. Hilarious.

"Don't worry. I wouldn't be seen dead in your hand-medowns. You took all the good stuff." She sits up straighter. "Actually, have you seen my denim jacket?"

"Er, what was that?" I wobble the phone around, so my face appears as a blur in the corner of the screen.

"Niamh. Did you take it?"

"Megs, you're breaking up . . . can't hear . . . frozen . . . love you, bye!" I disconnect the call and make a mental note not to post any photos where I'm wearing her jacket. I swing my legs down off the riverside wall and begin the walk back up to the Globe. I'm not in a rush to get back to the new dorms, and I'm hoping I can lose myself in a show at the theater. A rosy-cheeked lady there in a red apron exchanges my crumpled bill for a standing ticket and I follow the crowd into the circular yard of the theater. It's magnificent.

The set is minimal, but the actors are wonderful—so good that I'm glad there's no huge set to distract me from them. It's *A Midsummer Night's Dream,* a play I'm not familiar with, but the actors are masters of timing and the audience are enraptured. Before I can catch my breath, the company leaves the stage and intermission is announced. People begin to stream out of the courtyard to my left and right, which is when I spot a familiar figure in the thinning crowd.

"Tommy?"

"Niamh." For a second, a look of shock crosses his features, but it passes quickly and his face breaks into a dimple-licious grin. "Fancy seeing you here." He's dressed in jeans and a loose T-shirt, but it doesn't look quite right on him. Maybe it's because I first saw him in his museum garb. Weird, though, how he suited the old-fashioned stuff more. He gestures to the stage. "Enjoying the show?"

"It's wonderful," I say enthusiastically. "They're all so talented! That one guy is playing, like, three instruments, and . . ." I trail off as I realize how uncool I'm being, but Tommy smiles at me. "Yeah, I like it. I mean I've never seen anything like it. Well, I have seen plays, just not like this, you know?" Oh, God, stop talking, stop talking now.

"So we can safely say the answer is yes, then?"

I nod, pressing my lips together to stop any more word vomit from dribbling out.

"Good. It's one of my favorites."

"It's nuts," I blurt, then wince inwardly. Classy. To my surprise, Tommy bursts out laughing.

"You know, I think you're right." He leans toward me. "And you know what? It gets crazier."

"So, what did you think?"

Tommy hands me the ice cream that he insisted on buying and begins to walk toward the railing by the water. I follow him a little awkwardly and busy myself by unraveling the foil and paper wrapper.

"I loved it," I reply, taking a tiny bite of the ice cream. My teeth burn, but I feel all weird licking it in front of him, so I carry on with nibbling. "I needed the distraction."

Tommy turns and fixes me with a serious look. "I heard what happened to the girl in your class. That must be hard."

"Thanks," I say. "It was a pretty big shock. I've never seen a dead body before—well, not like that."

"What?"

"Sara, the girl in my dorm." Tommy's skin has turned a weird ashy gray color. "She was murdered. Sorry, am I freaking you out? I don't always talk about murder."

"A girl was murdered? Where you live?"

"Yeah. I thought that was what you were talking about. Who did you mean?"

He swallows. "The girl who should've been at the museum with you. Natasha, I think?"

"Oh, yeah." My shoulders sag. "Poor Tasha. I've not had much luck with friends since coming over here. Or actually, they've not had much luck since they met me."

Tommy surprises me by tucking a finger beneath my chin and lifting my head up. It's an intimate gesture from someone I hardly know, but it doesn't make me uncomfortable. Quite the opposite, in fact. "Hey. It's not your fault."

"I know." I don't even sound convincing to my own ears. "Let's change the subject, OK?"

"Agreed." Tommy bites the bottom of his ice-cream cone off and sucks the melted innards out before shoving the whole thing in his mouth and grinning at me with chocolaty teeth. "Your turn."

"What? No, don't be stupid."

He snatches the cone from my hand, but he underestimates my need for ice cream and I snatch it back from under his nose.

"Nice moves," he laughs, resting back on the railing. "So, when are you back at the museum? Tomorrow?"

I finish the cone as delicately as I can muster and fold the wrapper in my hand. "Day after. You?"

"I'm always around. What are you doing tomorrow, then?"

"Research, I guess. There's this scholarship for next year that I need to write an essay for. There's a lecture tomorrow that should help. I'll probably go to that, then camp out in the library."

"So you're planning on hanging around, then?" Is it just me or does he look the teensiest little bit hopeful?

"Maybe. I do love it here." As I say it, I realize that I do. Silence stretches between us as the city lights twinkle along the river. A cool breeze tempers the humid air, and despite all that has happened, I know I will do my best to stay.

"Are you sure you have to go?"

I glance at my phone, shocked to see it's almost midnight. I start to make a comment about pumpkins but manage to stop myself just in time.

"Yeah." I let the word hang in the air as Tommy stuffs his hands farther into his pockets. If he wasn't the prettiest human around, I'd think he was as nervous as me. "I have to be up early and it's pretty late . . . plus I don't really know the city yet."

"Can I at least walk you to the train?"

"Yeah." I guess I'll have to brave it at some point. "I mean, thanks. I'd like that."

"Good."

We continue to walk in silence for a couple of minutes, making our way back along the river, which now seems to have a thousand diamonds sparkling on its surface. I'm not certain where we are exactly, but Tower Bridge winks at me on the horizon, so I know we're on the right track.

"We're here." Tommy stops in front of a darkened coffee shop and points to a sign. "London Bridge station. You can get pretty much anywhere from here."

"Perfect." I smile. And I keep smiling. Dear Lord, I've forgotten how to use my words. I clear my throat and it comes out all horrible and hacking, not the ladylike way I was intending. "That's great," I try.

He takes a tiny step closer. I can feel the heat coming from his skin. It's cool out now, but he doesn't seem to notice, and I can't stop staring at his strong, sinewy arms. It's his turn to clear his throat. "So," he murmurs.

"Yeah. Home time." I hold my breath, unsure what to do as he inches toward me. His strong hand catches hold of mine and lifts it to his mouth, pressing a whisper of a kiss on the sensitive skin. My insides melt immediately.

"I wish I could walk you home." He lowers my hand and takes a step back, an unwelcome breeze carving between us and snapping me back to my senses.

"You can, if you want?"

"Oh, it's not that." He gestures back the way we came. "I live on this side, though, so . . ."

"Fair enough." I can still feel his lips tickling my skin and have to hold back from begging him to do it again. "See you in a couple of days, then."

"You will." He smiles. "I had a great time with you tonight, you know."

"Me too." I turn toward the station. "Bye, Tommy."

"Bye, Niamh."

I practically float to the redbrick entrance, where I pause, glancing back under the guise of rooting around for my Travelcard, but he's already gone.

I descend the steps, hot air wafting past me as I leave the street above. It's eerily empty down here and my footsteps ring on the tiles. I pass through the turnstile, feeling very Big City. The long, clunking escalator plummets into the depths, below the surface of the earth, where no one will find me. Jesus, I need to stop this, put the brakes on my overactive imagination. I hurry down the gliding steps and realize I've underestimated the height of this thing. I can barely see the bottom. I really hope there are other people waiting for trains down there.

I'm halfway down when the lights go out.

My head jerks back as the escalator jolts suddenly, stopping in its tracks. I struggle to see my hand in front of my face until my eyes adjust to the little emergency light way down at the bottom of the handrail. I try to focus on it, but it's there one minute and gone the next, replaced with darkness. Or a shadow.

I hear it then, from below me. The scraping of metal on metal. As though someone is dragging something sharp across the sides of the escalator. It's excruciating. The sound tears through the silence, and I could swear it's getting closer. The darkness is closing in, and I realize . . .

Someone is on the escalator with me.

I flash back to every stupid kung fu film my dad has ever made me watch and grip the rubber handrails on either side of me, put my weight into my arms, and blindly launch both legs out in front of me.

Nothing. My feet drop, clunking back onto the metal step. I pause, trying to breathe as quietly as I possibly can. The only sound now is my heart beating in my eardrums . . . until a long, slow scratch sounds on the metal panel directly in front of me.

Nonononono. I take a deep breath. Not today, Satan.

I kick out again, and this time my feet connect with a body, a gust of breath telling me I've hit my target. I throw my body backward before whoever it is can drag me down with them, my ribs crashing against the step's sharp edges. There's a muffled thud below and I begin to run blindly back up to the surface, climbing the steps two at a time until my thighs are screaming at me to stop.

Light sears into my eyes as the escalator moans back to life beneath my feet. It's undoing all my hard work, carrying me back down toward my would-be attacker. I brace myself, ribs aching, but ready for a fight.

Only, there's no one there.

I allow the escalator to carry me down the last few steps. I'm confused. Where did they go? I definitely just kicked someone down here, but there's not a trace of them. My feet follow an empty, curving tunnel, my eyes darting around the dirty tiles. A low, agonized whine starts to burn into my ears.

I stop abruptly, but I can see her around the next turn. A girl huddled into the wall, long, dark hair forming a curtain over her face.

"Hello? Are . . . are you OK?" Of course she's not OK. The girl doesn't move, so I gently clear my throat to try again. "Do you need help?"

She lifts her head. Ribbons of red streak down her face, a wide, hollow space pouring tears of blood into her hands.

I'm not sure which one of us screams first.

6

I hover my thumb over the screen. Just one click and that's it, boat booked. I could be back home in less than twenty-four hours.

"Niamh?" A kind voice interrupts my thoughts. "Are you OK, dear?" Ruth walks over to me, leaning heavily on her cane, its rubber tip dragging across the floor. I sigh and put down my phone, almost grateful for the interruption. My thoughts are as tangled as one of those big balls of rubber bands—a mess of a million colors strapped in different directions, each one piling on top of the last.

"I guess." I don't bother to smile. I haven't got the energy. I can imagine how awful I must look after another sleepless night, but I don't care. I swept my hair back into a rough ponytail before, and shoved on the first clothes I'd found in my bag. I pick at the ragged hem at the knee of my jeans, worrying the fraying edges and making the rip wider. Ruth lowers herself into the chair across the table and leans forward. "There is a counseling service here, you know. After everything you've been through this week, it might be helpful to talk to someone."

"Yeah." I keep my voice vague. I really don't see how talking to a stranger is going to help me. How could they understand any of this?

Ruth seems to read my mind. "Or you could talk to me?" she says gently.

I glance at her beneath my bare lashes. "Really?"

"Of course." She taps my phone screen. "If you decide to stay, that is."

The boat-booking page is still up on the screen. I let out a deep breath. "I can't decide. My parents . . . well, they're worried. Because those girls were attacked." I don't mention that they don't actually know about Tasha; Derek agreed to keep that one quiet.

"And you don't want to go?"

I chew at my bottom lip. "I dunno. I think I want to stay."

Ruth smiles at me, her eyes crinkling up. "I get where they're coming from, trust me. I have a daughter your age, you know. I'm keeping tabs on her too, believe me. But . . ." She sighs. "But I also know she has her own dreams, has to make her own mistakes."

"I don't know if they understand that," I say.

"Maybe you do need to be careful right now," says Ruth. "For your sake and theirs."

I frown. "What do you mean?"

"Two girls were attacked. You need to be sensible. Don't go out after dark, not too much, anyway. Walk with a friend, check in with me every now and then. Tell your parents you're doing all of that. Reassure them, for goodness' sake." She pushes herself up from the table with a groan. "Oof, achy bones." She smiles. "Now, don't you have a lecture to get to?"

I check my watch. She's right; the lecture starts in ten minutes, and I still haven't decided what to do. She reads my thoughts again.

"The boat won't be full in an hour, lovely, if that's still what you want to do." She nods at the door. "Go. Learn. Worry about this afterward."

My eyelids have never been this heavy, not even after the early mornings on Granny's farm. The lecturer's voice is a blur, each monotone word indistinguishable from the last. I pinch the skin under my arm in an effort to wake up, but the dark, stuffy room is fogging up my brain. I desperately try to concentrate on what he's saying. I need some information if I'm going to write this essay.

"Then we have the more traditional puppet shows of the Victorian era. You will, of course, know Punch and Judy. . . ."

Pictures flicker past on the large screen, but my mind is busy wandering back to last night and my eyes start to lose focus. The girl I found in the station had to have surgery. She lost her eye. A shiver crawls over my shoulder blades as I recall the scraping sound of metal on metal in the dark station, the gust of hot air that enveloped me on the escalator. I straighten my back and push myself up in the seat, desperately trying to think of something—anything—else.

"This character is known in various guises, such as the Devil, or, in one period of Victorian history, as a character named Spring-Heeled Jack. This ne'er-do-well could have been an exaggerated urban myth, or maybe a deeply disturbed figure responsible for brutal attacks on women in the city. Either way, he grasped the public imagination, and so the Devil became Spring-Heeled Jack for a while." The lecturer continues and I shake myself awake. Scholarship, Niamh. Words. Essay. If I'm going to write the damn thing at all.

I pick up my pen to take notes. My wrist brushes against the edge of my notebook and I'm back on the South Bank, Tommy's lips whispering against my skin. If I go home, I leave everything behind, including any chance I have with him.

Suddenly I have laser focus.

"That leads us nicely to penny dreadfuls and their influence on theater in Victorian London." Paper rustles all around me as everyone reaches for the handout I've pretty much forgotten about. I flip the first page. "These books contained a whole host of characters you may be familiar with and some you may not: Frankenstein's Monster, Jekyll and Hyde, and, of course, Spring-Heeled Jack."

A hand goes up somewhere toward the front. "Yes?"

"Which one is Spring-Heeled Jack? Is it this guy?"

"It is indeed." The lecturer presses his clicker and the screen shifts to a large version of one of the small black-and-white pictures on the handout. A man with a devilish beard is depicted leaping over a wall, his dark cloak spreading out around him. He's almost flying. "He was a bit of an enigma, old Jack. No one has ever discovered who he really was, if he was real at all, although there are many different theories. Not unlike his namesake, Jack the Ripper." The lecturer chuckles, his voice much more animated now, almost cheerful. Not creepy at all. "He dressed like a creature no one had seen before, white oilskin suits and blue flames shooting from his mouth." A ripple of laughter disturbs the quiet room and I find myself joining in. It does sound pretty ridiculous. "He was said to be able to bound over fences and even buildings. It was reported that he tore at the skin of young girls with metal claws, though he was never caught and we only have the tabloids of the nineteenth century to go off. . . ."

My hand shoots up into the air, almost of its own accord.

"Did you say metal claws?"

"I did." His eyes twinkle in the most unsettling way behind his thick glasses and he lowers his voice. "There have been sightings of him across the centuries, all the way up to the modern day." A shiver ripples around the room and he chuckles and changes the screen, which floods the room with warm light. "Anyway," he continues, "penny dreadfuls really catered to the lower classes, making theater more accessible. . . ." I stop listening as images flash through my mind.

Metal claws. The scrape of metal on metal. And a girl with blood running down her face.

7

I push the library door open, still breathing hard. The bell tinkles to announce my arrival.

"Ruth?" I shout, before remembering that I'm in a library. I try again in a whisper. "Ruth, are you here?"

There's movement up in the stacks, so I throw my bag on the table and head to the stairs. "Ruth?"

"She's not here." A low, male voice answers from deep in the stacks. A long shadow creeps across the floor toward me, and as much as I want to move, I'm rooted to the spot as the tall, lanky figure of Will, the library assistant, emerges.

"OK, thanks. I'll just go," I manage to garble. I turn on the spot, and slam directly into another warm body standing behind me.

"Oof!" The figure bounces back as I try to catch my breath. "Sorry, didn't mean to startle you." A girl around my age is straightening a pair of dark-framed glasses and smoothing down a preppy checked skirt. "You OK?"

"Yeah, um." I glance behind me, but the boy has already melted back in among the books. "Yeah," I repeat. "Sorry."

"No problem. Are you looking for my mom? Ruth, I mean." She leans forward and lowers her voice, pointing back toward the stacks. "Ignore Will—he's a bit, well, a bit of a weirdo. Or eccentric, as Mom says."

Funny, that's what my mom would say. Always PC. I agreed with this girl, though—he freaked me out too.

"Ruth has popped out," she says. "But maybe I can help? I'm Jess, by the way."

"Thank you."

She heads back down the steps, her shiny, sun-streaked hair bouncing around her head. She has gorgeous, tight curls, tiny ringlets that have been carefully smoothed and separated. I follow her over to the circulation desk.

"So, what can I do for you?"

"Do you have any newspapers?"

"Sure." She cocks her head and snaps her fingers, the click loud in the empty room. "That accent is fabulous. You must be the Irish girl? Niamh, isn't it?" I nod reluctantly. "Mom mentioned you." She laughs and rolls her eyes. "She always seems to think I need a new friend." I nod again, not quite sure whether she's happy Ruth thought we could be friends or not. "What were you after again?"

"Newspapers," I repeat.

"Oh, of course! Today's? Or old ones? We've got some scanned, but the really old ones are on microfilm. We'd have to wait for Mom to come back to use that."

63

"Today's are fine, thanks." For now. Old newspapers could be interesting later on, so I store that nugget of information in the back of my mind.

"Cool, here you go." She pulls a sheaf of newspapers from beneath the counter and slides them across to me. "Gimme a shout if you need anything else."

"Thanks," I reply absently. The headline emblazoned beneath the red masthead of a tabloid has grabbed my attention.

LUNATIC ON THE LOOSE!

"Scary, isn't it?" Jess gestures toward the picture below the headline and I realize it's familiar to me. Tatty, yellowed wallpaper frames a door that is crisscrossed with blue-and-white police tape and signs that scream CRIME SCENE: DO NOT CROSS.

Sara's room. My could-have-been room.

If I had eaten anything today, I'm pretty sure I'd feel sick right now.

"You know," Jess continues, and I decide she's as big a gossip as my sister, "two of the girls attacked were meant to be starting the theater course here." Her eyes spark with interest. "What course are you doing?"

"Erm." I look down at the newsprint. "Journalism," I blurt.

"Oh." She looks disappointed and I breathe a sigh of relief. "OK." I pick up the papers as she seems to lose interest in me, and settle myself at a table. I glance behind me to see what Jess is doing. She's perched on the end of a counter, a thick book wedged in her hand. I subtly turn my back so she can't see what I'm doing.

Right. I spread the newspapers across the desk in front of me and scan the headlines, looking for anything that mentions an attack on a woman, discarding those that don't seem to have anything useful in them. I'm left with a stack that mention, among other attacks, the two that I witnessed this week, though no others mention unusual blades, as these ones do. I begin to flick through each of them, pausing every now and then to make notes. After about twenty minutes, I have a full page and fingers that are covered in newsprint.

Oh, and the beginnings of a conspiracy theory.

"What you looking at?" Jess's head pops over my shoulder and I jump in my seat, almost bashing her in the face. "Oops, I keep sneaking up on you, don't I?" She scrapes out the chair next to me and drops into it, placing her open book facedown on the table. Stephen King, a bit dark for me, but Meghan loves him. "Eww, the attacker with metal nails. It's so creepy."

"I know," I mutter, placing my forearms on the notebook to hide it.

"It's happening all over the city. That's crazy." She is right; aside from Sara and the girl in the station last night, police had linked two other teenage girls, speculating that they were all attacked by the same person. One escaped relatively unharmed, just cuts around her neck where her necklace had been stolen. Jess narrows bushy brows beneath her glasses as she looks at my page of notes. "Why are you so interested in all of this?"

Her voice is curious, rather than disapproving. I make a snap decision.

"I know—well, *knew*—two of them." I point to a grainy photograph of Sara that the tabloid has clearly lifted from her Instagram. She is beaming, a perfect smile in a perfect face. "I traded rooms with her when I got here."

"Wait," says Jess, her eyes growing wide. "So that should have been your room?" I nod. "Wow, you are a lot more exciting than Mom made you out to be. She just said you were lonely."

"I'm not," I protest, thinking of the way Tommy kissed my hand. "I have friends."

"I'm not saying—"

"It's fine," I interrupt, my voice curter than I intended. "Ugh, sorry." I sigh. "It's just been a horrible week already."

"Yeah." She studies me from behind her designer specs. "I'll bet. Listen, I'm sorry, you seem really nice, and . . ." I wave a hand to stop her.

"Honestly, don't worry." An uncomfortable silence settles around us. Then Jess leans over and whispers in my ear.

"She tried to set me up with Will once."

"What?" I squeak, laughter bubbling out of me. "Are you serious?" She nods.

"Yeah. So, I'm always a little bit wary when she tries to introduce a new BFF."

"I don't blame you." I giggle, which sets her off, and within seconds we're both clapping hands over our mouths so he doesn't hear us. I eventually stop and wipe my blurry eyes. "Ah, I feel mean now. But he is pretty creepy."

Jess nods, wiping her glasses on her sleeve before replacing them on her face.

"Oh, he'll be fine. Anyway, despite the brush with death, you seem pretty normal."

"Compared to Will?" I laugh, and we're in danger of losing it again. I catch sight of the newspapers and stop laughing. Jess glances down too, and her face becomes serious.

"Jeez." She pulls one of the papers toward her and studies it. There's a timeline of the victims with photos alongside on the open page. She looks down and then back at me. She does this three times before I decide I can't take it anymore.

"What?" I mutter.

"They, well . . ."

"What?"

She turns the page around so that I am looking down at it. "They all look like you."

I look at the parade of teenage girls with long dark hair. All have a smattering of freckles. I gently stroke the ones on the bridge of my nose. A bitter taste floods the back of my throat, and my next words barely reach a whisper.

"I know."

8

I drag myself out of bed early the next morning after another unsatisfying night's sleep. I've always had vivid dreams—nightmares, even, though I have plenty more fuel for them now than I ever did before. It's my day at the museum and I'm looking forward to distracting myself from thoughts of serial attackers and creepy Victorian myths.

Unfortunately, the museum is full of the latter.

It's only just past opening time and Geoffrey and I have the place to ourselves. I don't see Tommy and I'm too embarrassed to ask Geoffrey. Maybe he doesn't start till later. I wonder what he does when he's not working here, apart from going to the theater, that is. In the meantime, I'm trying to get to know the place, which means following Geoffrey around and letting him give me a history lesson.

Now he stops in front of a narrow booth that reeks of musty velvet and bad decisions. A faded poster, edges soft and tattered, declares it was once home to "Madame Josephine, the most gifted fortune teller in London Town."

Next to it is a display case crammed with what Geoffrey would call curios. A dusty spotlight draws my attention to a lone cushion, its golden tassels moth-eaten but otherwise well-preserved. A pale porcelain hand sits lightly on top of it and I edge closer, the fleshy mounds and crenellations beckoning to me in the creeping light.

"What's this, Geoffrey?"

"Oh, yes." Geoffrey removes his top hat and places it carefully on the glass case. He slides open the door and picks up the hand, cradling it gently. "You can hold it. It was once a fortune-telling device, popular in this era. If you look closely, you can read the original markings."

The hand is cool, delicate, and disturbingly lifelike in my own. Geoffrey is still talking, telling me what each line represents and how each finger relates to an element, but I can't concentrate on any of that. The museum shrinks away from me as a strange sensation shoots up my arm, a hundred tiny arrows that restrict my chest and puncture my windpipe. I gasp as a cool, mineral taste chokes the back of my throat and I forget that I'm holding something delicate, something almost two centuries old; I just want the damn thing away from me. I drop it quickly into Geoffrey's waiting palm and the world rushes back like a slap to the face.

He doesn't seem to have noticed anything unusual.

"Yes, yes, quite a charming little item, isn't it? We have all sorts of occult objects here," he twinkles, seemingly unaware of how unsettling his artifact is. "Ah!" He fixes on something behind me and straightens up. "Our first tour group has arrived. Are you ready for your debut, Miss Jane?" An echo of unease follows his words and I shudder. "I know you are shadowing me today, so I don't expect you to answer any of the questions and whatnot, but please do excuse me if I become carried away and introduce you."

I nod mutely, convincing myself that what I feel isn't actually fear and foreboding, but nerves. I've never acted in such close quarters before.

"Wonderful," he announces, replacing his hat and striding to greet his audience. "Good morning, dear friends," he booms. "Happy tidings to you all."

I follow the group on their tour. Geoffrey presents his version of a Victorian gentleman, which is pretty wonderful, plus he knows just about everything about the museum, so they are rapt.

We soon approach the dressing room, where the portrait of Jane Alsop is displayed. My palms are damp and sticky, but I'm not sure whether it's because of the lingering feeling of dread or because I know Geoffrey is going to try to make me join in now. My skirt whispers across the stone floor as I wipe my hands on it, desperate to clear my throat. I put up with the choking feeling instead. I'm not quite ready for the attention, not yet.

Thankfully, when we get there, Geoffrey gives me a look that seems to say "Ready?" and I shake my head no so fast, I almost pull a muscle. My shoulders release as he tips me a tiny, knowing nod and carries on, all without breaking his stride.

"This room was thought to belong to a wealthy young lady who lived in the home attached to this building, the daughter of the factory owner. Not much is known of her life, though we do have records of both her birth and untimely death."

My ears prick up.

He gestures to the picture behind him. "This portrait of Jane Alsop was commissioned shortly before her sixteenth birthday, as was common at the time. The Victorians liked to commemorate a significant life event in some, ah, unusual ways. Please, come closer." The crowd, including me, step forward as one, tethered to his story. "You can see a few of the details are missing. The lace detail on her sleeves, some of the curls in her hair. They were left unfinished. The portrait—abandoned."

"Why?" a young man asks, one hand wrapped loosely in his partner's. Something catches the corner of my eye and I see Tommy in my peripheral vision. He's looking as enraptured as the rest of us, although he must have heard this story a thousand times.

Then I realize his attention isn't on Geoffrey; it's on me. My cheeks flame and I'm grateful the lights are dimming again. I adopt what I hope is a casual pose and pretend I haven't seen him. Be cool, Niamh.

"There was a terrible accident." Geoffrey's voice is low, and I have to strain to hear every word. "Much is unknown, although the death certificate does confirm the horrific way poor Miss Jane died."

One of the kids in the crowd eyes me warily and edges away, looking between my costume and the painting. I make a mental note to surprise him around a dark corner later on.

"However, details emerged over time, adding up to a tragic story of forbidden love and untimely death that has survived alongside the artifacts. There were rumors at the time that Jane had a secret love, a young man who worked on the factory floor. Someone, of course, who she would have been forbidden to marry, due to her father's high social status."

I dart another glance at Tommy. His gaze is fixed on Geoffrey. I don't know whether I feel relief or disappointment that he's lost in the story, not looking at me anymore.

"That's so sad," murmurs a woman in a raincoat. A quiet rumble of agreement ripples through the crowd.

"Yes, yes, it is." Geoffrey sighs and hooks his thumbs through the lapels of his topcoat. "And the story gets only more tragic, I am afraid. Jane crept down to the factory floor one evening, probably to attend a rendezvous with her paramour."

"Or to meet her man, in other words." Tommy's sudden whisper in my ear makes my heart speed up, equal parts surprise and pure delight. I choke back a laugh and fight the urge to lean my weight back into the warmth of his body, now right behind mine.

"It is presumed that they were together—perhaps, ah, *distracted*." Tommy nudges me and I bite my lip, but when I glance at him, I see that his eyes are sad. "It is thought that Miss Jane's hair somehow became tangled in a machine, and her death certificate suggests that she was dragged toward—or rather, into—the mechanisms of a cotton spinner." There is a sharp collective gasp from the crowd. Geoffrey continues with relish. "Her mangled corpse was recovered the next morning."

Talk about being able to hear a pin drop. Poor Jane. "So he just left her there?" The woman in the raincoat speaks again, her tone now dampened with tears. "Her lover?"

"It is thought that he fled," Geoffrey says. "In their society, it would have certainly meant the workhouse for him, or worse. Not that there was much worse." He looks around, delighted at the downcast faces. "Shall we continue?"

The crowd begin to follow Geoffrey to the next shopfront, his voice booming again, as if he hadn't just told the saddest story ever. I stay where I am, studying the incomplete parts of Jane's portrait. I didn't notice them before, but now they're all I can see.

A vibrant, promising life cut short. Just like Sara and maybe even Tasha, though I hope not. There's been too much grief and sorrow already.

"I bet her boyfriend was heartbroken, having to leave her like that," I say to Tommy, but there's no reply.

I turn around and realize I'm alone, with only fragments of a dead girl for company.

9

I greet Jess at the entrance to the museum. She shakes off her umbrella and steps inside, wiping her feet on the rough welcome mat. The frames of her glasses are rose-petal red today and match her lipstick. Turns out she's a real history nerd (her words, not mine) and once she heard about this place, I couldn't keep her away. Rain streaks down the outside of the frosted-glass doors, allowing me little glimpses of the world outside. The warm, damp smell of the city follows her in.

"Hey," she says, greeting me in return, dumping her umbrella in the basket by the door. "It's miserable out there. Oh—wow!" Jess catches a glimpse of my costume and attempts a whistle, but it comes out as more of a splutter. "Oops," she laughs, dabbing her lips on her sleeve. "Still can't do that."

She chatters brightly as I lead her through the turnstile, and it feels good to allow my shoulders to loosen. I try to let her excitement chase away the darkness of this morning.

"I can't believe I didn't know this was here!" She squeals in delight as we step into the cavern, only to be silenced by a pointed look from the raincoat lady from the tour earlier. She's been here for hours now.

"You'll know more about all this than me, though," I say to Jess. "You're the history expert. I don't have a clue about any of this stuff."

"Hardly." She brushes it off, but I see her flush with pleasure at the compliment. "So, are you going to give me the tour?"

"I'll try." I lead her around the cobbled street, taking her into the stores, which we can enter. There's an old-fashioned sweetshop, full of glass jars of sherbet lemons and licorice. There's even a lingering hint of cocoa in the air. There's a hatter's too, where Jess whips out her phone and we pose for selfies in bowler hats and frilly bonnets, vogueing in front of an ornate mirror. I try my best to remember Geoffrey's speech from this morning and point out the bits that come to me, but I'm hardly doing it justice. Jess interjects when she knows something, and I quickly discover that she really is a bit of an expert. Her passion for the past is evident in each word.

I avoid the fortune-telling booth, hoping she won't notice. Her gaze does linger on it longingly as I pick up my pace, but the rope that bars the entrance keeps her away. I'm not sure what it is about that corner, but my skin crawls just looking at it. Thankfully, Jess lets me lead her past.

"This is amazing!" Jess stops just short of pressing her face against the side of another exhibition case. I don't remember seeing this one in detail, actually—Geoffrey said that he likes to mix up the tours a bit. It must be boring doing the same thing over and over. I wonder what else I've missed.

The cabinet is made of glass, tall with sliding doors at the front. The shelves are glass too, and they display a collection of jewelry and other random bits and pieces. Most of the other displays have a theme, but I can't see one here right away. It doesn't look hugely exciting to me, but Jess seems enthralled.

"I've never seen anything like this in real life, have you?" Jess breathes.

"What, like rings and brooches and stuff?"

"Well, obviously I've seen jewelry before." Her voice drips with friendly sarcasm. "But these aren't just *any* rings and brooches, are they?"

"What do you mean?"

"Ah, I see you have found the mourning section." Geoffrey's unexpected boom makes me jump. "Is this young lady a friend of yours, Niamh?"

"Yeah." I introduce Jess and they shake hands in a very formal, English way. "Is that OK?" I didn't think about whether I was allowed visitors; it's a free museum, after all. I hope he's not annoyed that she's here.

"Of course! It is your lunch break, is it not?" I nod. "It's just wonderful to have young people in here; I often wish more would stop by."

Phew.

Jess starts asking questions that are way over my head, so

I let them chat while I take a closer look for myself. *Mourning display.* It's funeral stuff.

I scan the case as I try to follow their chatter. One layer is clearly clothing and textiles. There's a pretty black handker-chief, a gauzy square made from lace with bows and flow-ers decorating the finely woven, delicate edges. A small box sits next to it, about the size and shape of a box of matches, with slim black pins spilling out of it. It is emblazoned with a crest and the words *Black Mourning Pins.* The information card next to it explains how women would wear black when their husband or another family member died, and mourn-ing pins because silver dress pins weren't suitable. Jeez, they took the whole mourning thing pretty seriously in those days. There is also a series of haunting mounted photographs (or "daguerreotypes," as I hear Geoffrey tell Jess) of somber, veiled women in huge black gowns.

A shiver runs down my spine as I look into their blank expressions. Creepy AF.

I move my attention to the next shelf. A necklace made of thick, shiny black stone, labeled as jet, lays so heavily on the shelf that I expect to see dents in the glass. There are tiny seed pearls embedded into its hanging pendant, their swirling arrangement forming the shape of some dearly departed's ini-tials. Small diamonds are sprinkled along its base, hanging to delicately mimic the tears of the family members left behind. It is morbidly beautiful.

I am examining a delicate locket containing a tiny oil

painting of a young boy when Jess's voice interrupts me. "What's usually here, Geoffrey?" She's pointing to a bare shelf, where a card says the artifacts are out on loan.

"Ah." Geoffrey's voice is tinged with sadness as he lowers it to a baritone whisper. "I'm afraid that is a slight fabrication. These objects are not on loan—they're missing. You see"—he lowers his voice further—"the items on this shelf were stolen a few weeks ago."

"Stolen? Really?" I ask. Jess looks at me as though she forgot I was here.

"Yes, but don't worry, my dear." Geoffrey chuckles sadly. "Events like that are thankfully quite unusual, I must say."

"Were they valuable? Like, rare?" Jess asks.

"Not particularly." Geoffrey smooths his neat white beard with one hand. "Fascinating items, as all of them are, but not valuable. They sell similar on that extraordinary eBay website."

I swallow a smile—he makes eBay sound like it hasn't been around for decades already.

"What was stolen, then?" Jess presses.

"More mourning jewelry. One or two old pamphlets on mesmerism—that's hypnotism, you know. An 1830s cigarette lighter, quite a beautiful thing. Very unusual, indeed—more akin to a gas lamp than a modern lighter. German, I believe . . . Ah, do excuse me!" Geoffrey ambles over to an older couple that has been hovering.

My stomach is rumbling and I've had enough of creepy

artifacts. "C'mon," I say to Jess. "Let's go for something to eat. I'm starving."

But Jess isn't listening. Her eyes are drilling holes into Madame Josephine's booth instead. The red velvet rope still blocks the entrance, and I now see that a sign reading NO ENTRY hangs from it.

"Not yet. I just want to look in there, then we'll go. OK?"

I fumble for a response. I don't want to go near the booth.

"I think it's off-limits, Jess. Look, it's blocked off."

"Nah, Geoffrey will let us have a peek," she says firmly. "He loves talking about this stuff. Look, he's finished with those people now."

"You go, then." I plaster what I hope is a smile on my face and give her a little elbow nudge in his direction. "I'll go and get changed. . . ."

"Geoffrey?" Jess ignores me and her voice echoes through the cavernous space. His head twitches in our direction. "Can we have a look in there?"

He beams. "Why, of course."

Goose bumps erupt on my arms. I look around to see if there is a visitor I can excuse myself to speak to, but the place is deathly silent. Tommy must be on his lunch break too.

Geoffrey ambles toward the booth and unclips the rope, removing the "No Entry" sign in the process.

"After you, ladies." He pushes against the entrance to the booth and it swings inward, a dark room lying beyond. It's not just a little fortune teller's booth, after all. It has been adapted, like one of those secret rooms in a library I've always dreamed about. It's a doorway.

Jess grins at me in triumph.

"See?" she whispers, grabbing my hand. "I knew it would be awesome. Come on."

My feet are glued to the cobblestones. "I don't know. . . ."

"Please?" She gives me full-on puppy eyes and I sigh.

"Fine."

"Yay!" She drags me beyond the rope and into the chalky darkness.

Inside, my skin prickles under the thin fabric of my costume. We are standing in a small room, barely large enough for the three of us to coexist in. Geoffrey fiddles with a panel on the wall and a low buzz breaks the silence, dusty yellow lights blinking lazily, as if waking from a deep sleep. They illuminate a bank of glass cabinets along the bare brick wall that is filled with an assortment of items, and Jess makes a beeline toward them as I hang back, that horrible spiky feeling permeating my bones again.

"What is this place?" I ask, more to myself than anything. Geoffrey beams.

"This, my dear, is the infamous Madame Josephine's parlor. Fortune teller, hypnotist, and mistress of the occult."

"Cool," Jess breathes. "Is this it? I mean"—she trails a hand along the cases—"I thought there would be more stuff."

"Ah, yes." Geoffrey runs a hand over his beard, pressing his belly into his topcoat. "You recall the robbery I mentioned? Well, I'm afraid this space bore the brunt of it."

"Why?" My voice is loud in the barren room.

"There were several unique items here. Some, we are lucky enough to still have." He steps closer to the case. "This, for example, is a rare, early tarot deck. Tarot started life as a game in France, did you know that? The Brits thought of the French as more . . . mystical, shall we say."

I edge forward reluctantly, whereas Jess almost pushes me out of the way in her excitement.

"Sorry." She grins.

I study the upturned card, careworn and soft, balancing on the rest of the deck. Beside it is a threadbare velvet case. The card is horribly beautiful, there's no doubt about it. It is mostly black, clearly hand-painted, and there are traces of gold leaf clinging to the central figures. The image on the card is of two skeletons, intertwined, locked in an eternal embrace. I glance at the lettering at the bottom, faded and cracked. *L'Amoureux.*

"The Lovers," Jess whispers.

"Now, over here we used to have something very special." Geoffrey is standing by the central case. "It was said to be Madame Josephine's grimoire. We only have a photograph of it now."

"Grimoire?" I repeat.

Geoffrey unlocks the cabinet and slides the photo out, holding its edges delicately before handing it to me. I raise it to the dim light and Jess comes closer, her loose hair tickling my neck.

The picture is of an old book, its cover brown and

dog-eared. Crude markings are carved into the ancient leather—some kind of stars, from what I can make out.

"What's a grimoire?" I ask again.

"A book of magic, right?" Jess says.

"Very good." Geoffrey's voice is gravelly. "This was a very rare example indeed. Grimoires such as this were not found in Britain until the late nineteenth century, and this"—he taps the photograph with a manicured fingernail—"this was a French original, possibly passed down through generations. Until Madame Josephine brought it to London with her, that is, sometime in the 1820s." He looks at me, and his gaze becomes unfocused. "They say, young Jane, that there was even a spell to resurrect a lost love—if one had the right items . . ." He pauses, his smile flickering from wolfish to grandfatherly in a split second, so fast, I'm not sure it really happened. I laugh nervously, placing the photo back in the cabinet.

"Good thing I'm not Jane, then, isn't it?" I choke out, his slip with the name unnerving me. The clatter of feet in the museum behind us announces the arrival of the next tour group, and Geoffrey is immediately distracted.

"Please excuse me, ladies." He tips his hat to Jess, who doesn't seem to notice anything wrong. "Niamh, could you return in one hour? You can continue to watch the tours for the afternoon session."

"Yeah, sure. Thanks." I try to shake off the uneasiness and focus on something else. Like the fact that I'm still starving. I turn to Jess. "Know anywhere cheap for lunch?"

She is still frowning at the shelf where the grimoire should be. She raises her voice and calls after Geoffrey. "What was the jewelry in the other cabinet like, Geoffrey?"

I sigh dramatically, pointing to my wrist and feigning dying from hunger to hide my nerves. He pauses in the doorway, his tall figure blocking out the light. "A keen mind, indeed, young Jess. It was more of the usual, I'm afraid. Miniature portraits, initialed rings—oh, and those bracelets and brooches common to that era. The ones made of braided human hair."

10

I stab the last fry with my tiny fork, its splintering wood piercing the soft, soggy flesh. It's stuck right at the bottom and I have to drag it up the side, scoring noisy white lines into the polystyrene cone as I bring it closer to my mouth. I pull it to the top in triumph, swollen with vinegar, just how I like it. The acid burns my tongue and I lick my lips, all coated in salt. Perfection.

"That was a good chipper." I swing my legs down from the riverside wall and hold out a hand for Jess's trash.

"Chipper?" Her eyebrows knit behind her glasses.

I dump our garbage into the nearest overflowing trash can and wipe greasy fingers on my jeans. "We call the chip shop the chipper at home."

Jess shrugs. "I might steal your word, it sounds so cool in your accent." Ah, here it comes: the moment I've been dreading. "Chipper, chipper, chip . . ."

"Stop." I clasp both hands over my ears, mock offended at

Jess's butchering of the Irish tongue. "Please, stop! I can't take it!" We grin at each other, on the verge of laughter, ready to launch off the precipice, just not quite there. Jess's face softens.

"Wanna talk about it?"

I let out a deep belly sigh as I position myself back up on the wall, my palms lightly grazing fragments of stone and seashells. I pick at the clear polish on one fingernail. It's already chipping, so it peels off easily, in one sheet. I roll it between my fingers.

"It might help, you know."

"I know."

"Or," she says, reading my thoughts in the same eerie way her mom did earlier, "we could talk about something else?"

I lift my head to meet her eyes and force a smile. "That sounds better."

"So . . . Boyfriend? Girlfriend? Pet cat?"

I shake my head, although I can't help thinking about Tommy and his dimples. "None of the above. Next question."

"Come on," she presses. "There must be someone at home."

"God, no. We live in the middle of nowhere. The only guys I get the chance to see in real life are either related to me or feral. Usually both."

"Eurgh, that's depressing. We'll have to introduce you to someone here."

I nod in agreement but can't quite stop the smile that is spreading across my face.

"Wait, have you met someone you like already?" she demands. "Spill."

"There's a boy. Tommy," I confide. "At the museum. We had a kind-of-accidental date the other night." I fill her in and she laughs when I tell her about the hand kiss.

"That's kind of cheesy."

"It wasn't. It was . . . perfect." I glance at her. "What about you?"

"Next question, please."

"Seriously?" Jess nods. Her expression is tight, and I sense it's more complicated than she's letting on. "OK, OK, no love life stuff. Got ya."

"Thank you." She shuffles toward me, closing the gap between us and pulling her phone from a tiny backpack. "So, while you were getting changed before, I Googled the museum robbery."

"Oh, yeah?" I say, trying to sound enthusiastic. The unsettling display creeps back into my mind. "Find anything?"

"Nothing online—I guess it's not major news. I mean, it's hardly groundbreaking. But then I found this." She hands me her phone, pointing to a tiny, blurred article, as if someone has taken a photo of the corner of a newspaper page. "It was on one of the library archive sites; I used Mom's password. Anyway, it lists all the things that went missing. Stuff like this." She takes the phone and taps quickly, her thumbs both flying across the screen before handing it back.

It's a random Pinterest board, but nothing like the ones I've made in the past, when Meghan and I wanted to redecorate our bedroom, or my list of free things to do in the city. Instead, there are tarnished silver rings topped with tiny coffins, black-and-white photos of people who don't look particularly, well, alive, and a long glass vial filled with liquid. I squint and see that the label says *Mourner's Tears*. My God, Victorians were dramatic.

Oh, and creepy, I decide, as I scroll past a small doll, its white face and hands the only color on a sea of black. She's wearing a mourning dress and veil, and beneath her tiny, rosy cheeks, a portrait of a man rests across her chest. It's framed in bronze and a winged skull sits on the top. Clearly not a child's toy, then.

"This isn't the actual stuff that went missing, but I'd say it's pretty similar. Fascinating, isn't it?" says Jess.

"Horrendous, more like. Who would want to steal this?"

"Who knows? Keep going, though, you haven't gotten to the creepiest bit, yet."

Seriously?

I sigh and keep scrolling. There's a whole selection of brooches on the screen now. All are in that sepia tone of old photos. Some show crisscross patterns, others tiny paintings of graveyards or weeping willows. A couple of others contain portraits decorated with ornate wreaths.

"They're . . . kind of pretty, I guess?" I say, desperate to hand the phone back. "The wreaths."

"Look closer." Jess has a devilish glint in her eye.

I do. It takes a moment, but when I'm looking back at the braided material, I suddenly see it for what it is.

My fries threaten to make a reappearance. "Is that . . . ?"

"Yep."

87

It's hair. All of it. It's braided and woven, weaved into pictures and decorations, shades of browns and yellowed blond, faded red. It's all human hair, taken from people who have died.

Dead-people hair. "Weirdly cool, right?"

I barely hear her. My vision has started to swim and there are tiny sparks of light flashing in my eyes, pinpricks climbing up my hands and feet. I slide off the wall like a limp piece of spaghetti and huddle into a ball, my back pressed up against the safety of the concrete, my arms wrapped around my knees. A wave of nausea sweeps over me. I try to cover my face, regulate my breathing, wondering whether I've eaten something bad.

A gentle hand on my shoulder grounds me and the pins and needles recede a bit as Jess's voice cuts through the buzz in my ears.

"Hey, it's OK, breathe. I think you're having a panic attack. In through your nose and out through your mouth." I try to follow her advice, sucking a deep breath in. Oxygen fills my lungs. Better. I force it out and heave another in, snorting loudly, but I'm far from caring. The world begins to refocus so I carry on, following Jess's soothing tone as she repeats herself: in, out, in, out, in . . .

"Better?" My head weighs a ton as I lift it to look at her. She's crouched beside me, her normally light brown skin pale in contrast to her bright lips. "Has that ever happened before?"

"No." I carry on taking deep breaths as Jess helps me up

to my unsteady feet. She rummages in her bag and pulls out a half-full plastic water bottle, unscrews the lid, and offers it to me. "Drink this."

I take the water and gulp it down gratefully, my mouth Sahara-dry after all those deep breaths. I sag against the wall. The water seems to rehydrate my brain so much that it's now pressing against my skull, trying to find a way out. I can feel the mother of all headaches coming on.

"Thanks." I roll the empty plastic back and forth, letting it crack and crunch between my hands. "How did you know what to do?"

Jess waves a hand. "Mom has them sometimes. Because of the MS." Ruth? No way; she seemed so calm.

"MS?"

"Yeah, that's why she walks with a stick. How are you feeling?"

"Wobbly." I try a smile, but my mouth just twitches. "Damn, I'm supposed to be back at the museum. What time is it?"

"It's fine, you've got fifteen minutes. Are you sure you want to go back, though? I'm sure Geoffrey wouldn't mind if you went home to bed."

I weigh the thought. My head is thumping, but I don't think I'll be able to sleep. It's more likely that I'll lie in bed, alone, replaying the last few days over and over in my head. No thank you.

Maybe I should take Jess's advice about one thing, though. Maybe talking will help.

I take a deep breath.

"So, all that disgusting hair jewelry. When I saw it, I dunno, I guess it kind of gave me a flashback or something."

"Of what?"

I spill out the horror of the last few days to Jess. To her credit, she sits and listens quietly, rather than running away screaming.

I tell her all about finding Sara, her open, staring eyes and the way clumps of her hair had been torn out at the root, an image I know I'll never be able to shake off. I tell her about making friends with Tasha and then her being attacked. I tell her about my close call in the station, the metal screech that is etched in my brain. Finding the girl on the platform, her hair hanging in front of her face, the gaping wound where her eye had been.

Jess's smile has vanished by the time I finish. She looks a little sick but determined.

"Right," she says, zipping up her bag and swinging it over both shoulders. "We're going back to the museum to tell Geoffrey you don't feel well, and then you're coming home with me." I start to argue, but she doesn't give me a second, grabbing my hand and pulling me away from the river, back toward the museum. "Nope, no excuses."

"OK," I say meekly.

We walk along together in silence for a while. Jess seems deep in thought. At last, she says, "You see what all of these attacks have in common, don't you?"

"Yeah," I say glumly. "All the girls look like me."

She stops then and gives me a look that is part sympathy and part concern.

"They don't just look like you, Niamh. I think the attacker thinks they *are* you."

11

"Just two minutes, I promise." Jess drops her backpack and disappears behind the library counter. She's going to ask Ruth if it's OK for me to sleep over.

A large, open book on the big desk catches my attention. It's as big as one of those giant newspapers that my granddaddy used to get on a Sunday, full of different sections that he'd spread all over the farmhouse table. I take a furtive glance around. I can't see anyone. Maybe it just hasn't been put away yet. I'm sure Ruth won't mind if I take a peek.

I walk over for a closer look. The pages are mottled and the binding looks heavy. Leather, maybe. The edges of the paper (or was it parchment when it was this old?) are brown and ragged, worn with age. They remind me of when I made a treasure map for a school project once, Meghan and I carefully stained paper with wet tea bags and stole a lighter to set the edges on fire, burning a hole in Mom's favorite tablecloth.

I trace a finger over the page and try to decipher the

writing, but it's old-fashioned and pretty hard going and my head is still killing me, so I look at the pictures instead.

Just for once, I'd love to stumble across something cute, like a picture of puppies frolicking or that one of two otters holding hands so they don't drift away from each other.

But no. Crudely drawn illustrations of a grotesque figure stare up at me and I shudder as I recognize the world's creepiest puppet, Mr. Punch. His large hooked nose is unmistakable, curving to meet a prominent chin on his roughly hewn face. He's holding a bat in his tiny T. rex arms and has a huge, manic smile.

There is another figure in the picture too, a creature with two curled horns, a small pitchfork and a billowing, black cape, drawn to appear like a bat's wings. He's also smiling, but it's way more sinister, the twist of his mouth so sharp it almost splits his face in two. I try my best to focus on the handwritten caption below and a memory resurfaces from earlier in the week, from the lecture about theatrical history in London. The other character must be the Devil.

"What are you doing?" The voice in my ear is quiet but gravelly, harsh.

"Nothing!" I spin around and bump into the person behind me, sending an explosion of books through the air. "Oh, I'm so sorry!"

I go to help him pick up the books, try to gather them back, but the boy who works in the library—Will, I remember— glares at me so hard, I back away. He snatches them up quickly and holds them to his chest.

"You should be careful, Niamh," he says.

I didn't realize he knew my name. And why do I have a horrible feeling he's not just talking about being careful with the manuscripts?

The books he is carrying are similar to the one on the table: old, leather-bound, gold writing engraved on the spines. I see some of the titles: *A History of the Penny Dreadful, Victorian Mourning Rituals.*

One more book still lies on the floor and I stoop to pick it up. *The Story of Spring-Heeled Jack.*

"Hey." For a second I forget that this dude completely freaks me out. *That's* why I remembered the lecture; the Devil character in Punch and Judy was replaced by Spring-Heeled Jack for a while. Spring-Heeled Jack was some kind of Victorian supervillain who stalked women through London, wearing metal nails and . . .

"Give me that." I wince as Will rips the book from my hand. He quickly ducks away, his skinny body vanishing around the stacks, holding his books tight.

But not before I see his hands. A clear, angry line of crescent moons are carved into the flesh on the backs of them.

As though someone has been clawing at him.

Between the air-conditioning in the café and the chills still licking at my spine, I can't seem to get warm. I clasp the paper cup of tea in my hands, steam rising lazily, little curls and wisps of heat that are fleeting and gone. *Sugar for shock,* Derek had said.

I think I'm going mad. Everything that has happened, not to mention the sleep deprivation, would be enough to send anyone loopy, surely. I lift the cup to my mouth, but I don't drink. Instead, I close my eyes, inhale the comforting aroma of a good cup of tea, and let my eyes fill with tears.

I want to go home.

"Hey." Jess plonks down on the bench in front of me. "I wondered where you'd gone." Her voice softens as I open my eyes and a lone tear spills down my cheek. "Hey, don't cry. Is your head still bad?"

I nod. It's easier to let her think that my headache has caused this second meltdown. God, she must think I'm high-maintenance.

"Here." She hands me a white packet. "Mom gave me them for your headache. Take two," she instructs. I pop two little pink pills out onto my palm, toss them into my mouth without question, and hand the packet back.

"Thanks," I mumble. Sugar coats my tongue as the shell begins to melt on contact, and I wash the tablets down with a mouthful of scalding tea.

"Ready to go? You still want to stay over, right? I mean, you don't have to. I'd *like* you to, but if you'd rather not—"

"Jess," I interrupt. "I can't think of anything worse than going back to a room on my own right now." I attempt a watery smile. "If you don't mind hosting a whimpering wreck, I'd love to sleep over."

She grins. "Cool."

There's a stretch of comfortable silence before I give in

and start to talk. I think about my encounter in the library. "How well do you know Will?" I ask.

"Not very, thank God." She picks up my abandoned plastic lid and swirls it around on the table with one finger. "Why?"

"I dunno, I just get a bad vibe from him or something."

Jess nods slowly, as if considering my words, but then shakes her head, her nose scrunching.

"Nah, I think he's pretty harmless. He keeps to himself, really."

"Sure." I can't stop seeing the marks on his hand, though, as if someone had desperately been trying to fight him off. Recently too—they were fresh and raw. Should I mention it? What if I'm wrong?

What if I'm right?

"Listen," I begin. "I saw Will in the library just now, and . . ."

"No. That's not possible."

I blink at Jess. "Yes, I did. I bumped into him and he dropped all these books, and that was when I saw—"

"Whoa, slow down!" Jess holds up the white lid like a stop sign and I take a breath. "He's not working today. His name wasn't on the log-in sheet."

"You checked the log-in sheet?"

"No, it's on the door to Mom's office. Makes it obvious who's on shift."

"Oh. Well, he was there, I know it!" I tell her all about the encounter, and once I start, I can't stop, it's all pouring out of me like a leak, even though I sound like a complete idiot.

"OK, give me a minute." Jess steals my cup and takes a sip of tea, pulling a face when she realizes it's more sugar than liquid. "So you think this Spring-Heeled Jack character might be connected to the attacks?"

"Well, it sounds stupid when you say it like that." I sigh. "But maybe, yeah."

"And Will had cuts on his hands?"

"Defensive wounds, yeah."

"Niamh, not being funny, but how do you know what defensive wounds look like?"

I mumble a response.

"What?"

"*CSI,*" I say, louder, and Jess starts to giggle. "Look, I know how it sounds, but they really did look like someone had been trying to push his hands away."

Her laughter subsides.

"You really are serious, aren't you?" I nod, scared to say any more. "OK then, come on." She stands up. "We're going back to the library."

"What, no, I . . ."

"It's fine," she says firmly. "Mom will be there, and if Will gives us any trouble, she'll know about it. And if he's gone, then I know a way to figure out what books he was looking at. It might help us make sense of this. Either that"— she hesitates—"or we'll have some kind of theory to take to the police."

12

Back in the library, there's no sign of Will, not even a stray book on the table. We offer to hold down the fort for Ruth while she runs some errands, and as soon as she's gone, Jess types Will's name into the database.

"This should list every book he's borrowed." She frowns at the screen and I peer over her shoulder. It's a list of Sherlock Holmes and Agatha Christie novels.

"Couldn't he just take them off the shelves? I mean, there wouldn't be any need to scan them out that way, would there?"

"I guess." Jess slams down the mouse in frustration. "They could have been anything, then, from any part of the library."

I try to remember the titles. "There was one about Spring-Heeled Jack, one about penny dreadfuls, and a big one." I stretch my arms out wide to indicate the size of the large book that was on the table. "Huge. Like a scrapbook, all old and worn-looking."

"A folio?"

"Er, yeah?"

Jess snaps her fingers in triumph. "They might be in the Victorian collection! Did they all look old?"

"Yeah, leather-bound with gold writing on the spines." Jess nods happily and begins to tap at the keys. "Recognize any of these titles? *The Rise of Mesmerism, Reading the Tarot, Victorian Mourning Rituals* . . ."

"Wait! He definitely had that last one. I remember it because of all that awful hair stuff you showed me this morning."

Jess frowns. "He's been in Special Collections, then. Oh, and—this is weird—what's that Jasmine girl's last name?"

"Taylor, I think. Why?"

"Look." Jess points at the screen and I see that *Taylor, Jasmine* was signed into Special Collections earlier this morning.

By William Letki.

"Will let her in. That's suspicious—only Mom should have access to the archive rooms."

"We are supposed to be doing research, though. Your mom mentioned Special Collections the first time I met her. Isn't that where all the rare books and stuff are kept? Maybe she told Jasmine about it too."

"Yeah, maybe. She doesn't let just anyone in, though—the stuff is really valuable. It's like a big, cold vault." Jess shivers. "I don't really like it in there, but needs must . . ." She rummages around under the desk before producing something the size and shape of a credit card. "At least he had the sense to put the spare key back." She wiggles her eyebrows. "Ready to enter the crypt?"

No, no I'm not, I think. But I keep my mouth shut and follow her anyway.

"This place is crazy. I've never been in one of these before."

My voice bounces around the cinderblock enclosure as we approach a mammoth gray wall that stretches up toward the ceiling. Jess flips a switch and the lights flicker on fully, revealing that it is split into sections, each decorated with a large black wheel.

Jess consults one of the laminated signs stuck onto the metal and chooses a wheel, taking hold of it like the captain of a ship. I expect a loud screech, but the mechanisms all move smoothly, obviously cared for, and the expanse of metal in front of us begins to part, creating a small, dark crevice.

"Cool," I whisper.

"Yeah." Jess keeps turning until the yawning space is slightly wider than the two of us and stops, tilting her head as a bell jangles in the distance. "Oh, dammit, that's someone in the library. I better go and see what they want; Mom will lose it if she knows I'm in here again."

"Again?"

"Yeah." Jess talks over her shoulder as she hustles to the door. "She had to rescue me at Christmas. I came in without telling her and locked myself in. She completely freaked out. There's no cell reception in here, so she thought I'd gone missing, or something, so . . . Oh, don't worry!" Ah, so the look of horror on my face *is* totally obvious. "Look, I know you're here, and I'll only be five minutes, OK? I'll get rid of whoever it is as fast as I can. You make a start." And with that, she leaves the room.

I remember she has the only key a beat too late, so when I dive for the door, it clicks shut in my hand. Damn it. I twist the handle, but it's like I thought—it locks from the outside. Brilliant.

She'd better come back soon.

I turn to face the gaping maw of the strange rolling shelves. It really is dark in there.

"Maybe I should just wait right here." My voice echoes and rolls around the empty space, seeming to disappear down the corridor of shelves, the books sucking up my words. Jesus, pull it together, Niamh. I straighten my shoulders and take out my phone, turning on the flashlight. It's not been the same since I had it fixed. They definitely used some cheapo parts, but it gives out just enough light for me to see down the row—just books, neatly arranged on shelves, nothing to worry about. I glance back down at my phone, seeing that Jess was right—no signal to speak of—and realize my shift at the museum would just be ending.

I wonder if Tommy noticed I wasn't there this afternoon.

I physically shake the thought of him from my head and focus on the task at hand. I pad over to the first shelf. None of the books look familiar; in fact, most seem to be handwritten, like diaries. I work my way down to the darker end of the wall. I have to hold the flashlight closer here, in order to make the golden titles flash, give up their secrets. I focus on one that I think looks familiar and ease it from the shelf, but my phone wobbles and the light is hidden for a moment.

It only takes that split second to realize the main lights have gone out.

Again.

It's like I'm a magnet for electrical problems. I fumble the book and my phone, panic rising, when I realize I'm going to drop one of them. I grasp the phone tightly, my only source of light slick under my palm, and the book hits the floor with a muffled thud that may as well have been a thunderclap. The little light dances crazily. I lift my head and that's when I see it.

There's a shadow blocking my way out.

"J . . . Jess?" My voice is barely more than a croak. "Ruth?" I try again, but the same thing happens, my tongue sticking to the roof of my mouth. "Is that you?" I whisper.

The shadow doesn't falter, and I begin to think that it's just a trick of the light, something to do with the books and the way the big ones are stacked up. Or maybe it is Jess.

"Jess, is that you?" My voice sounds a little more confident, but I stay rooted to the spot. I'm not going any closer until I know who—*or what,* my brain adds unhelpfully—is there. "C'mon," I try, though I'm pretty sure she wouldn't pull something like this. "Not funny."

The shadow melts away.

"Hey," I call, my legs no longer cemented to the floor. "HEY." Anger fills my voice, the last few days of fear turning into something more solid and raging. "Leave me alone!"

There's no reply, of course there's not. Hot tears slide down my cheeks, burning right through the temporary rage. I scramble on the floor and my fingers curl around the book I dropped. As far as weapons go it's not ideal, but it's better than nothing. I shut off my light and feel my way instead, inching along the space between the shelves. I don't want this cretin to know where I am.

My skin shrinks on my bones when a high, metallic scratch pierces the silence.

I freeze, trying to keep blind panic at bay—I can't afford another panic attack right now. Forcing myself to think calmly, I start to list what I know about the room.

There are no windows in here. No phone service or Wi-Fi. There's only one door in and out, and as far as I know, Jess has the key. I can't scream; *it* would find me before anyone came, even if I could be heard through the thick walls. I try to recall what the ceiling looks like—is it full of those little tiles, the kind in movies that hide tunnels and stuff? This room is kept cool, to protect the books, Jess had told me, so I guess there could be air-conditioning vents up there. I'd have to climb the shelves, though, and they're metal, so again I'd be giving away my position if I even tried. . . .

The piercing sound of metal on metal starts up again, but this time it's got a weird kind of rhythm, almost like they're making patterns in the metal, drawing circles. A gentle breeze raises goose bumps on my bare arms, and I realize what the sound is.

Someone is turning the wheel.

"No." My voice is a strangled whisper as I forget all about making noise. A draft rushes around me now, the closing shelves forcing the air out, creating a vacuum for the books. I stretch my arms out.

I can touch both sides already.

I stumble forward, dropping both my phone and the book this time. I don't care, I just need to get out of here. The room is so utterly thick with darkness that I seem to be swimming through molasses, my body moving in slow motion. Something tickles my neck and I jump. It's just a book.

But it's a book that is way too close for comfort.

"Please." I'm begging now, all pride long gone. "Please."

The scratching stops for a second and I try to run, but I'm already stuck, large folios on the bottom shelves barring my exit. I turn sideways and edge along. The noise starts up again, so close now that I know I'm near the opening.

And then I am so nearly out, I hurl my body through the closing gap, but my leg becomes caught and before I know it, the metal ridges of the shelving are pressing painfully into my back. I yank at my leg until something pops, white hot pain searing through my ankle. I don't mean to cry out. I clap a hand to my mouth a fraction too late and strain my ears to listen for movements, but the room is still.

Someone is banging on the other side of the door. "Niamh? Niamh! Open the door!"

"Jess!" I scream. "Jess, there's someone in here, please, you have to help me!"

"But you have the key!" she wails. "The key is inside."

"No!" I yell. "I don't have it. Jess? Jess?" No response.

"No, no, no!" I pull at my foot again and this time it releases, sending me sideways into open air so that my head is free of the shelving.

That means my face is right next to the wheel.

A featherlight scratch traces a path down my cheek and I freeze. It carries on, cool metal curving beneath my chin, then grazing up the other side of my face. My eyes fill with horrified tears, but the touch isn't painful or punishing.

It's gentle. Almost loving. A caress.

"Hurry up, Mom, please hurry!" Jess's voice bleeds through the door and suddenly a dazzling beam of light sears into my eyes.

I can just make out a vague, blurry shape moving past me, and then the door opens, and I see Jess and Ruth and I don't care about anything anymore. I close my eyes.

I'm safe.

13

Déjà vu.

Only, not really. I've definitely been in this situation before, but this time I'm no longer the witness. I'm the "victim."

I hate that word.

"So." Detective Moran, the detective interviewing me, glances at his notebook. "You say that you were alone in the, ah, Special Collections room?"

I nod, casting my eyes down guiltily and trying to avoid Ruth's gaze. She reaches over to squeeze my hand, her heavily ringed fingers closing over mine. She looks tired, her skin ashy and pale.

"It's fine, Niamh. Just tell them what happened. All that matters is that you and Jess are safe."

"But I've already told them everything!" I wrap the thin, police-issue blanket tighter around me, struggling to warm up. The cool air drafts remind me of the library. I bet the police do it on purpose: crank the AC right up just to unnerve people.

I shift in my chair (which is so uncomfortable, it surely breaks several of my human rights) trying to redistribute my weight without jarring my left foot, which is currently propped up and covered with an ice pack. One butt cheek is completely asleep, so it's tough, but I manage. I wiggle my toes experimentally and am relieved that, despite the definite twinge in my ankle, everything seems to be in full working order. The EMT said it was a bad sprain but not a break.

It's damn sore, though.

"I'm sorry, Miss Hughes." Detective Moran sighs, scratching his salt-and-pepper stubble. "This is procedure. I know it might be difficult for you but, well, we seem to have a situation on our hands." More hot tears streak down my face, my skin already tight from crying, and his gaze softens a little. His eyes are bloodshot too. "Really, Niamh, your statement will be a huge help. No one else has been able to provide us with a proper account of what happened, not since the beginning."

I look up.

"Beginning? You mean Sara?"

"Uh, no." Detective Moran flips back to the start of his notebook. "There was an attack on June twenty-seventh. The young woman survived, but she was badly shaken. She was walking home from . . ."

"June twenty-seventh?" I interrupt him again and he clears his throat, irritated.

"Yes."

My mind whirs. Late June—I was still at home then! I didn't even arrive here until the middle of July. Some of the tension in my shoulders begins to unravel and I feel lighter than I have in a while.

I can't be the link, after all.

"Niamh?" Detective Moran's voice nudges me back to the present. "Is everything OK?"

"Yes, yeah, it's fine. I'm fine." I take a deep breath. "I'll tell you what happened as best I can."

And I try, going over every little detail I can dredge up. Brains are weird, though; what was once so clear is now a hazy mash of heightened survival instincts and pure horror. The actual events have been diluted and I'm already sifting through the events, starting to assign a rational explanation to each part.

"And you said that the perpetrator touched you?"

"Yes." This is one memory that still has the power to bring up bile from the pit of my stomach.

"On your face?" The detective mimics the movement with his blue pen, the chewed end tracing a path down his rough cheek.

I nod.

"You don't have any visible marks, though. In fact, you only suffered one injury." He gestures to my elevated foot. "Why do you think he left your face uninjured?"

I shrug, still cold despite the blanket. How should I know?

Detective Moran leans across the table, shifting his empty coffee cup out of the way to show me his notes.

"First victim: Mary Stevens. Injuries to the face and head. Second victim: Sara Mondrial, deceased. Injuries to the face, head, and neck. Third victim: Natasha . . ."

The heavy metal door of the interview room crashes open. I realize I've physically recoiled from Detective Moran's words, now all curled up and small in my chair.

"That's enough!" a voice booms as someone comes through the door.

I don't know what I was expecting, but it wasn't this.

"Derek?"

"Sir." I stare as Detective Moran leaps out of his seat to address the older man. What the hell is going on?

Derek nods at Ruth and fixes his eyes on me, completely ignoring the detective, who sinks back down into his seat.

"You all right, Irish?" he says. I nod mutely. "Getting yourself into all sorts of trouble, I hear." He stalks around to the other side of the desk and peers at the notebook over Detective Moran's shoulder. "Shame on you, Pete. She's a young girl. You're scaring the jeepers out of her."

"Yes, I'm sorry, sir, I was just trying to . . ."

"Less of the *sir* nonsense, Pete. I'm retired and all the better off for it."

"Yes, of course, s—Derek." He says it hesitantly, like a child calling a teacher by their first name.

"What are you doing here?" I manage to ask. The adults

in the room all turn to look at me in surprise, as if they've forgotten I'm here.

"Told you before, missy, didn't I? I'm your legal guardian while you're under the care of the college."

I look at Ruth, bewildered, who nods in agreement. "He's right. Derek's been looking after students here for the last two years. Part of the university's safety scheme."

"Trying to," he mutters, glaring at Ruth. "How could you leave them in that library all alone?"

"They weren't alone, they were in a building full of students and staff." Her voice is calm, but there's a wobble to it. "I would never, ever—"

"Stop." I massage my tight forehead and the scratchy blanket slips from around my shoulders. "Am I done now? Please? I just want to sleep."

Derek walks over and places both hands on the back of my chair, glaring at Detective Moran—Pete—over my head until he sighs.

Detective Moran flips his notebook closed and looks at me. "Yes, fine. But if we need to speak to you again . . ."

"You come speak to me," Derek says firmly, before gesturing for Pete to help me up from the chair. "C'mon, Irish, let's get you home."

14

"No way! So the guy running your dorms is a retired detective?"

"Yeah. It was brilliant. He put Moran right back in his box." I grin into the little screen, happy just to see my sister's face. She has her phone propped up on our shared dresser and is playing with her hair, curling it into ringlets and admiring herself in the mirror. "Where are you off to?"

"Nowhere, just bored." She wraps a long, dark lock around the metal barrel and fixes me with a look that I can feel all the way from Ireland. "So, when are you coming home?"

"Don't start, Megs."

"OK, OK, but let's get serious for a minute. Let's say this killer is after you. What if next time they succeed?"

"They won't."

"You don't know that." She lets the curler loosen its grip, a ringlet springing up around her face, and starts the process again on a fresh section of hair. "I want you to come home in one piece, you know."

"I know." I watch as she curls two, three, four more sections of hair, an easy silence between us, even though I've barely spoken to her for a week. "Megs, I need you to do something for me."

She puts the curler down and looks at me expectantly.

"Why do I feel like this won't be a good idea?"

"Just listen." I take a deep breath, knowing that if she agrees and something does happen to me, she'll never forgive herself. "I need you to pretend to be Mom."

"What?" She picks up the phone, and for a second, I see flashes of our familiar bedroom. My stomach clenches.

"If the police or Derek call home, I need you to pick up the phone and pretend to be Mom."

"But why?"

"They might call and ask some questions, that's all. And then Mom will know. I'm just being cautious. I'm not ready to come home yet," I add quietly.

"Fine," she says. Her expression is worried, but she forces a smile. "But you let me borrow *anything* I want when you come home . . ."

"Sure."

"From your *London* wardrobe."

I grit my teeth. "Fine."

"Great! Dying of boredom over here. It shouldn't be too hard." She hesitates. "Mom and Daddy are busy with Granny H again."

"Oh, no, not again. What happened this time?"

"She went a bit loopy at the home. Doctors said she was dehydrated, which she was, but turns out she also had an infection. She hadn't drunk properly for days, so they had to sedate her to put a drip in. You know what she's like."

"I do." Poor Granny.

"Anyway, they've been rushed off their feet between work and visiting her." Meghan smiles proudly. "I've been cooking the dinners."

"Good girl." I smile.

"Yeah, I'm hoping if I keep the house nice, they might let me go see you after all."

Something like ice trickles through my veins. "Megs, I don't know. . . ."

"Fine. I guess I'll just have to tell them how much *fun* you're having." Her voice drips with sarcasm and I curse myself for training her so well.

"Oh, shut up. Just keep yourself out of trouble, OK?"

"Says you." She sticks her tongue out and I see the room blur as she throws herself back on the bed. She now has one huge, curled mop of hair on one side of her head, and the other is poker-straight. "Right, I'd better go. They'll be back in a bit, and I've got to put the potatoes on. Talk soon?"

"Of course." She plants a big, squelchy kiss on the screen, her lips filling it. I do the same, guilt beginning to gnaw at my tummy. "Love you, Megs. And thanks."

She waves it off. "Yeah, yeah. Love you too. Stay safe. Byeeeeeeee—"

The screen goes dark and she's gone.

I copy her, flopping back on my own bed in the new room. It's smaller than my first room—the one I never slept in. The view's awful too—a parking lot and some office buildings. Gutted. I stare up at the grimy ceiling, my eyes tracking the grid pattern of the tiles. It would be so easy to go home now. Jump on a boat or the next cheap flight and go back to normal.

But that was what was wrong with my life, wasn't it? It was too "normal." Boring, in other words. And, my God, have I worked hard to get here. All those shifts at the café after school, the farm jobs on the weekend. All that time and money spent on drama lessons, traveling to the city to audition. Will I have to give it up just because some creeper is stalking me?

Well, yeah, probably. It would be the sensible thing to do.

I let my imagination take over. What if I do write the best essay and win the scholarship? I can see it so clearly—my life in London at college, working at the museum, Tommy . . .

Tommy. I let my thoughts linger there, picturing his charming smile. If I stayed, maybe we'd have a chance, maybe even a relationship. I imagine future us standing on the South Bank, Tower Bridge all lit up in the background. Behind us, the Thames is dark and imposing. Tommy's lips are soft, gentle as he leans closer, brushing them softly across mine. . . .

Yeah, I'm not going anywhere yet.

It's hot in here. I kick my slides off, wishing I had been allowed to stay at Jess's after all—I'm in desperate need of some distraction and I could really do with the company. Will she still want to be my friend after all this? I hope so. I flick through my contacts and reach her name, hovering my thumb over it before I push.

Then I press the call button and wait patiently as it rings. And rings. And rings.

No answer. I decide not to leave a message because I seem to be sinking into the bed. The pillow is fluffy, like a cloud. I'll text her instead. I try to focus on the screen, but a yawn ripples through me and my eyes blur and water until all I can see is a bright rectangle. The phone slips from my open hand and I close my eyes, just for a second. I'll text her in a minute.

It takes me a second to remember where I am. Actually, it takes a second to remember who I am, what day it is, *and* where I am.

I push myself up from the facedown, drooling-in-my-pillow position and panic at the dark room—there is a distinct lack of light streaming through my window. I must have been out for hours. It feels like the middle of the night. Strands of hair cling to my clammy forehead and my mouth feels like something crawled into it and died. If anything, I feel worse than I did earlier, my head foggy and leaden. I pat around for my phone, finally disentangling it from the sheets. The screen is dark—out of battery. Damn it. My stomach rumbles a protest and I realize I haven't eaten since those fries at lunch. I try to ignore it, rolling over and squeezing my eyes shut, willing myself back to sleep.

It's no use.

I let my feet thump to the floor like dead weights and twist my body around so I'm lying sideways on the bed. I lie there for a bit and try to put my foggy thoughts in some kind of order.

One, pee. Two, charge phone. Three, food. My stomach rumbles again. Definitely food.

I stand up, stretching my arms out as wide as they'll go, trying to loosen all the kinks and knots. I switch on the light, shielding my eyes as the fluorescent bulb groans to life. Blurry-eyed, I wander into my little bathroom (the only perk of this new building) and when I come out, I stick my phone on the charge, grab a packet of instant noodles from my stash, and leave the room in search of hot water and a clean bowl.

These halls are quiet, but much more modern, so they automatically feel a little less creepy. I boil the kettle, idly wondering whether Derek is still downstairs or if it's the night watchman, the one who makes a little fort of comforters behind the desk so he can nap. The kitchen clock catches my eye: almost midnight. I really was out for hours.

I'm so hungry, I start slurping the noodles on the walk back. The hot, savory liquid scalds my lips, but it also cuts through the horrible cotton mouth. My sore tongue tells me I need to give it five minutes, though.

Once I'm back in my room, I exchange the bowl for my phone, which is now happily charging in the corner. Two WhatsApps, a bunch of junk email, and, I'm delighted to see, a missed call from Jess. I open the WhatsApps first: one from Jess, apologizing for missing my call, and the other from Meghan, to say that Granny H doesn't seem to be improving, so Daddy is staying at the hospital with her. They'll be too busy to worry about me, then. I shake my head and push the selfish thoughts aside quickly, feeling like a horrible child. Poor Daddy; he would be lucky if Granny H recognized him in the morning.

I retrieve my dinner and sit cross-legged on the bed, wriggling so my back is against the wall, and drag a pillow onto my lap. It hits me that my ankle hasn't bothered me and I stretch it out tentatively. It feels fine; I guess the ice did the trick. I blow on the noodles for a bit as I scroll through my social media, which is filled with friends at home who don't seem to have any Niamh-shaped holes in their lives. I tap in Jess's name and request to follow her. Then I click into the camera for a noodle selfie, ready to filter my lonely dinner for one and caption it with something that seems vaguely more exciting.

As I'm perfecting my "student life" pose, a dozen tiny thumbnails of photos load up. I pause, squinting at them. I expect to see the ones I took on the South Bank earlier today; I don't recognize these at all.

They're dark, nothing more than little black squares. Did I cover the lens by mistake? I click out of the app and into my photo album.

The forkful of noodles doesn't quite make it to my mouth.

I shove the bowl back on my desk, spilling hot broth on my fingers, but they're numb. Somewhere in the distance I hear the fork clatter to the floor. None of it registers because I'm scrolling through my phone, through hundreds of pictures, the same image repeated over and over.

An image of me. Here, in my room. In bed. Asleep.

15

I slam the phone down so hard that there's a chance I've shattered the screen again.

I must still be asleep, that's all. What do they do in films, pinch themselves? I try it, squeezing the skin on my calf. Ow. Not asleep.

I study every corner of my tiny room, my breath coming rapidly, but no masked murderers or camera-wielding psychos jump out from under the tiny desk. Everything looks so innocent—the room a bit sparse, a bit messy. Everything looks the same.

Apart from all the photographs of me asleep. My gaze travels to the bathroom door. It's slightly ajar. Didn't I close it before? Mom would go nuts if I didn't at home. *"You weren't born in a barn, Niamh."* But I can't remember. . . . I whip my feet up suddenly.

What if he's under the bed?

Right, I need to calm down for a second. I can hear my

heartbeat. It's thumping so loud that it's in my ears and I can hear all the blood swishing around in there too. I could just look under the bed . . . or in the bathroom. . . .

Or I could dive for the door and get the hell out of here. Option three sounds like a winner.

I leap from the bed like an Olympic gymnast and fling the door open, my bare feet hitting the hallway floor with a slap as I run toward the bank of elevators.

A soft click behind me lets me know my door has shut.

Or been opened.

I press the elevator button five, six, seven times, as if I can make it come any faster. The lights above me flicker. Not this again. There is no way I'm getting stuck in the elevator with some weirdo stalking around the dorms. I consider the door that leads to the stairwell, then remember I'm on the eighth floor now.

The lights flicker again.

Oh well, at least it's eight flights *down*.

I have to press my entire body weight into the door to open it. The stairwell beyond is exactly like the ones in every zombie apocalypse movie ever: buzzing overhead lights, bare cinderblocks, a massive sense of dread. . . .

A metallic tapping that I know too well sounds somewhere behind the closing door.

I fly down the steps as though the Devil himself is chasing me. At the bottom I burst out through the door, startling a snoozing Derek at the front desk.

"Derek! You're here, thank God!"

I try to gasp out a few more words, but I used every last breath running down those stairs. I lurch toward the desk, pointing over my shoulder while taking deep, sucking gulps of air. Thankfully Derek is already on his feet and moving toward me protectively.

"It's OK," he says, his eyes scanning me. "Take your time." I try to regulate my breathing as Derek assesses the situation. "What happened?"

I reach for my phone. Easier to show him. I slide my hand into my back pocket, but it's empty.

"My phone," I gasp.

He frowns. "What, did someone call you? What did they say?"

I shake my head. "No. I . . . I was asleep and when I woke up and checked my phone, there were all these pictures. . . ." My chest rattles as I take another deep breath. "Of me."

"Of you?"

"Yeah, but not like selfies, y'know? Pictures of me. Asleep."

Derek bristles. "What? From when?"

"From now! Well, from earlier tonight. I fell asleep and when I woke up, my phone was off, so I charged it, and . . ."

He doesn't speak for a moment. Then he says, "Where is your phone now?"

"I must have left it upstairs."

"OK. Wait there." He disappears back behind the desk

121

and doubt starts to scratch away at my fear. No one followed me down the stairs. There was probably nobody in my room. But those photos . . .

"Right." He emerges and tucks something into his back pocket. "Don't gimme those eyes, Irish, it's just a taser. Just in case."

Oh. Just a taser. Cool.

I trail behind him to the elevator and eye it doubtfully. "Was the electricity being funny down here?"

"No, why?"

The doors yawn open in front of us and I'm reminded of a recurring nightmare I used to have, where the pulleys all snap and I'm left swinging in an open elevator by one lone wire.

"The lights were flickering upstairs."

He looks at me with something like concern. "Probably just an old bulb. They're always going in a building this size."

"Right." I follow him into the elevator. It drags itself up slowly, juddering to a stop at my floor. His hand stays reassuringly close to the taser.

"OK," he says as we step out. "Your room. Come on."

My heart starts to thump again as we near the door. It's shut. Derek edges closer and does that classic police thing of putting his back against the wall. He nods at me.

"Ready?"

My tongue is stuck to the roof of my mouth, but I manage to choke out a yes. Derek swings the door open to an empty room. The bathroom door is still ajar, but he rips it open without hesitation. Again, empty. Relief floods my body.

"Clear," he says, and I start to giggle, all the stress of the last few minutes dissolving into hysteria. "Pull yourself together, girl. Now, where's this phone?"

My giggles subside. It feels off now that I know someone else has been in here. Less secure. Like my privacy has been completely invaded, which I guess it has. My phone is exactly where I left it, slammed facedown on the corner of the desk.

"Here." I unlock the device and hold it out to him.

"Er, no thanks, don't wanna be clicking through a student's phone."

"Oh. OK." I open the album and go to click on the last picture. It's one of Jess, swinging her legs on the wall with a mouthful of fries. I scroll through, but that's it.

"That's not . . . I mean, they were right here." I swipe through the other albums, thinking I might have been looking somewhere else, but the creepy photos are nowhere to be seen. Derek's sympathetic gaze burns into me.

"It was probably just a bad dream," he says. "You've had a hell of a time."

"No! They were here. Look!" I pull up a recently deleted file and expect to see multiple copies of my sleeping face, but there's nothing there, either.

Every single photo is gone.

16

"What, every single picture? There wasn't even one?"

"Yep." I slurp at the dregs of my chocolate milkshake before tossing the paper cup into a nearby trash can. I haven't had fast food in ages. Meghan always puts me off with those documentaries she watches, but she's not here and I'm exhausted and starving and a student, so it seemed like a great idea. And, not gonna lie, it was.

"Hmmm," Jess mumbles through a chicken nugget. She nibbles all the way around the edges, just like I do, and is busy working on the last one. I wait for her to finish before questioning her again.

"So, you believe me?"

"Er, yeah."

"Try to sound a little more convincing, will you?"

"No, I really do. I mean, the noodles were there, right?"

"Yeah," I say. "What do the noodles have to do with it?"

"Well, if you had a nightmare, and you looked at your phone *before* you went for food, you could've still been asleep and thought it was real. But if you were awake enough to go all the way to the kitchen, and boil a kettle and make noodles, and *then* you looked at your phone, it'd be pretty hard to do that while you were half asleep, wouldn't it?"

"Exactly!" Thank God someone is on the same page. "That's what I told Derek, but he wasn't having it. I bet he thinks I'm getting all hysterical."

"But he has a taser?" I nod in response. "Cool." Jess breathes.

"It is, right? He said I could move rooms so I'm closer to reception."

"Please tell me you took him up on that offer?"

"Hell, yes. The closer I am to him, the better, I think."

"Yeah, I think you're right." Jess pulls at a curl so it springs back up. "Do you really think he doesn't believe you?"

"I dunno. Ugh, you should have seen those pictures, though, just hundreds of them, all of me flaked out on the bed."

"You don't think he, when the creeper was in your room . . . ," Jess begins.

"What, did he sexually assault me?"

Jess nods.

"No." I cast my mind back. "No, I don't think so. So they're completely effing psycho, yes, just not in a sex-pest kind of a way."

"Well, that's kind of a bonus, right?"

I bark out a hollow laugh as we push through the glass doors at the entrance to the building. Jess is helping her mom in the library again today and I have drama workshops all afternoon, which I'm hoping will be ridiculous enough to distract me from all the trauma. Again.

"I don't know how you're going back into that library after yesterday."

"I wasn't the one who got trapped in the shelving units. Plus Mom's not been feeling great since. She's struggling to pick things up, so I'm going to be stacking shelves, mainly." She glances around and lowers her voice. "Also, Will didn't come to work this morning."

"Seriously?"

"Seriously."

"Holy hell." Was that because he was too tired from a night spent creeping around my dorms, taking and deleting pictures to make me look like a complete wacko? Or had he been looking out for Jasmine while she did it, convinced to help make my life miserable. I haven't seen her sneering face today, either.

Or was it just coincidence?

"Anyway, have fun at your workshops," says Jess. "You wanna meet here when you're done?"

"Yeah, please." I start to follow the mass of students trickling down to the drama studios. "I finish at five—see you then?"

"Yep, see you then." She waves goodbye as I allow the chattering crowd to carry me away.

". . . and the information will be outside the theater studio. I expect you will all apply."

What information? I realize I've just spent the last five minutes of my workshop totally zoned out. I'm so tired, you could pack for a weekend trip to Spain in my eye bags alone. I need to sort myself out.

I collect my stuff from the side of the room and zip myself back into the hoodie I discarded earlier. The class was actually really interesting. There was a lot of emotion recall, though, a technique where you remember past experiences to help you with a scene. I used the memory of seeing my sister in our messy shared bedroom back home. It left me feeling pretty tired and vulnerable. Still, I'm hoping a catch-up with Jess will make me feel better before I head home.

Home. Ha.

I spot a group chattering their way to the exit, and I follow them, hoping I'll find out what I missed at the end of class. They're talking about the scholarship essays and I relax. Thanks to Ruth, I actually had a head start for once.

Then I hear a familiar voice.

"Yeah, she woke up last night. I mean, I had to go and visit her right away; she's practically my best friend, you know?" Jasmine is just ahead of me with a handful of students, all hanging off her every word. So she made it in, after all. "She looked awful, poor thing, all bruised and battered. I felt terrible. I mean, that could have happened to me!"

Oh, please.

"So did she say who did it?" one of her cronies asks.

"Oh, I didn't stay long," she lowers her voice and I try my best to linger inconspicuously. "St. Mary's is a bit of a dive—I didn't want to hang around. I mean, we usually go private. I just dropped off some candies because she was sleeping."

"So you didn't even stay to talk to her?" Oops, did I say that out loud?

Jasmine's eyes flash at me. "Oh, it's you," she sneers. "I had somewhere to be, not that it's any of your business." She flips her silky hair over one shoulder and the buttons of her cardigan flash in the neon lights. It looks familiar.

"I bet you did. Hey, is . . ." I study the velvet edging and cropped sleeves. It is! "Is that my cardigan?"

"What are you talking about?" Is it just me, or is there a shadow of uncertainty behind her eyes? "This is my top."

"Prove it, then." The group falls silent, watching. I hear a whispered "Girl fight!" from the back.

Jasmine takes a step toward me, all uncertainty gone.

"Do you really think I would wear some trashy little backwater-town hand-me-down?" She lifts an arm and gives an exaggerated sniff, her pretty lip twisting in a sneer. "This can't be yours—it doesn't smell of potatoes." A few snickers give her a boost of confidence she really doesn't need. "Or desperation. I wouldn't be seen *dead* in something belonging to a hillbilly like you."

Tears burn my eyes as I try to think of a retort, but Jasmine turns away. She's done with me. I can still smell her minty breath as she addresses her entourage, as though nothing at all has happened.

"So, who's coming to Ben's party tomorrow? It's at this haunted theater, supposedly. I'll be able to tell. I mean, I am a very spiritual being. . . ."

Oh, for God's sake. I head out into the corridor, equipped with the only information I really need. Tasha is awake and at St. Mary's Hospital, wherever that is. I need to go and see her. I march away from the studios and back toward the foyer.

Jess isn't here yet. I fumble for my phone (which, to be quite honest, gives me the heebie-jeebies now, but I can't afford to replace it) and start to text her. I'm only halfway through a message when she appears in front of me.

"Jess!"

"Whoa, hi." She looks down at her arm and I realize I've grabbed her.

"Sorry." I grimace, unclenching my fingers.

"Has something happened?"

"Yes!" Her face tenses and I rush to explain, "Nothing bad, but yes, something has happened." She listens carefully, rolling her eyes as I recount Jasmine's nasty speech.

"Why would that horror bag go to visit Tasha?" she says when I finish.

"I dunno. I wondered that too." Just so she could brag about it? Guilt? Or for a more sinister reason?

"Well, let's keep an eye on her. Anyway, back to Tasha: if she's just woken up, I bet she'll still be in ICU."

"What's ICU?" I ask.

"The intensive care unit." Jess glances at her watch. "Visiting used to be six to eight in the evening. It's probably still the same."

"How do you know that?" Jess shrugs, so I tap the details into Google and see that she's right. "I thought you could just go at any time?"

"No, some wards have certain hours. Do you think they'll let us in to see her?"

"Who knows? It's worth a try, though, right? Maybe she saw something when she was attacked."

Jess nods. "Let me just run back to the library and tell Mom we're going to the movies or something. I don't want her worrying."

"OK." As she runs back toward the library, I feel a seed of unease start to bloom. I don't like lying to Ruth after everything that has happened, especially if it gets Jess more involved in whatever the hell is going on. I start to go after her, but when I reach the library, she is already shutting the door behind her.

"Done." She soon returns with a smile, linking her arm through mine. "C'mon. Let's go and get you some answers."

17

A tall—well, actually not that tall for London, but huge by my county's standards—building stands in front of us. It makes me feel depressed just looking at it.

"I know Jasmine is a snob, but I see what she means. It's kind of a dump."

"Yeah, it is a bit grim from the outside, I guess," Jess agrees. "Inside's not bad, though, and the staff are amazing. Jasmine clearly doesn't know what she's talking about. Anyway, all the royals have their babies here."

"Seriously?" I follow her around the side and we duck under the small blue porch at the main entrance. It drizzled all the way here and I refused point-blank to get on the train, making poor Jess walk. "How do you know all this stuff?"

"Mom was in here for a bit."

"Oh, God, Jess—I'm sorry!"

"Don't be silly." She waves a hand and her nail polish sparkles in the dim light under the scaffolding, all silver and gold glitter. "It was a while ago. In fact, it was when Kate Middleton was in having the second kid. Or maybe the third one, I can't keep up. Didn't get to see her, though. Mom's got epilepsy and sometimes her medication can interfere with it and cause fits, but she's been stable for a while now."

"That's good," I reply. Wow, profound of me.

"Yeah." Jess consults her watch. "So, ten past six—you ready to go in?"

I hold up the shopping bag that's crammed with sweets and trashy magazines. "Yep."

We enter through the sliding-glass doors and approach a curved reception desk, where a large, formidable woman sits behind a computer. She completely ignores me.

"Um, hi." Nothing. I clear my throat nervously and she looks over the top of her glasses. "Excuse me, I'm looking for the ICU. Please."

"Ninth floor," she barks, and I'm invisible again.

"Ninth floor," I repeat to Jess, rolling my eyes.

The hospital is bustling with people walking in and out of different doors, some chatting, some grim-faced and sobbing, others making earnest phone calls. I've never really been in a hospital. There was that time my cousin tried to pick me up when I was a toddler. He dropped me straight on my head and split my eyebrow open. I don't remember it at all, but it's gone down in family history, and we take a photo to recreate it every year. Families are weird.

We walk toward the elevator bank and a little kid presses the button excitedly. I smile and let my attention wander as we wait. My gaze snags on a slim figure in a baseball cap, leaning against the wall behind us, watching me. His (or is it her? Don't assume gender, Niamh) face is in shadow, so I can't make out their features, though I can feel the piercing gaze from here. I nudge Jess.

"Don't look now, but that person in the hat is giving me the creeps." To her credit, Jess does a half-decent job of not looking too conspicuous as she turns to see.

"Where?" she murmurs.

"Th—" The word dies in my throat as I look around.

There's no one behind us at all.

The kid in front of us cheers as the elevator arrives. We shuffle in behind his family and Jess asks him to press our button. He beams.

I say quietly, "There was someone watching us."

"You need some sleep." Jess gives my arm a squeeze. "I'm sure they weren't watching you. You're just on edge."

"Yeah." Even to my own ears, I sound pretty unconvinced. "Maybe."

We emerge from the elevator and approach yet another desk in silence. There's a nurse behind this one and I'm glad to see she's smiling as we approach.

"Can I help you?" she says. I wonder what it would be like to work here every day. I don't think I'd be so cheerful.

"Hi, yes, we're here to see Tasha." She tilts her head to one side, her smile frozen.

"Tasha?"

"Sorry, um, Natasha. Natasha Moss."

"Family?"

"No, just, er, friends. We're in the same drama course. I heard she'd woken up, and . . ."

"Oh." Her smile has dropped completely. "You're one of those." She clearly met Jasmine yesterday; she hadn't been lying about visiting, after all. "I'm not sure your visiting would be a good idea."

"Please!" I plead. "I've been so worried about her. I brought some magazines and stuff." I brandish the bag and try for puppy-dog eyes. They work on Daddy.

"All right," she relents. "Just for a few minutes."

"Thank you! Erm, where is she?"

"Room four, second door on the right."

"Thanks a million." I turn to Jess, who's pumping anti-bacterial gel onto her hands from a dispenser on the wall. "Ready?"

"Yep." She holds her hands in the air, like a surgeon about to go and operate. "You should do yours too." I follow her lead, rubbing the gel into my hands, wearing the plastic bag around my wrist like a bracelet.

Room four turns out to be a ward. The paper curtains are closed around most beds—I count six all together—but a couple are open and I can just about make out human forms under the starched white sheets. It's deathly quiet, except for the occasional mumble of families visiting loved ones inside the makeshift cubicles. A whiteboard on the far wall matches names to numbers, all scrawled in a marker that's on the verge of running out. I go and look at it and see that Natasha Moss has been allocated to cubicle five.

We pause outside her closed curtain. Jess is playing with her hair again.

"What's up?" I whisper.

"I've never met Tasha. Maybe I should wait out here until you see how she is?" she says awkwardly, and I nod. Awkward is a new look on Jess.

"Um, hi, Tasha?" I call lightly through the curtain. No answer. "Tasha? Are you awake? It's Niamh."

"Niamh?" A faint voice croaks from behind the curtain and I take it as an invitation to find the gap and peek my head through. She is awake.

That's about the best thing I can say for her.

"Hi." I force myself to plaster on a smile. "I was so glad to hear you were awake! How are you feeling?"

"Not great." She wheezes a laugh and pushes herself into sitting. "Could you hand me another pillow?" I grab one from the nearby chair and give it to her. The bandages on her arms blend into the white pillowcase seamlessly and she takes the pillow, tucking it behind her head. She winces at the movement. "Thanks. Sit down."

I do.

"I . . . Sorry." She frowns at me. "My memory is all over the place. But I know you, right? You were the girl who spilled the Coke on me."

Great.

"Er, yeah. It's Niamh. Sorry about that."

"Don't be silly. Least of my worries, wasn't it?" She tries for a smile, but her bottom lip is split and she winces as it pulls at the delicate skin. "I remember the name. Did you lend me the top I was wearing?"

"Yeah, that was me!" If she remembers that maybe she could help after all.

"They took it off me when I arrived. The nurse said she left it here, but she can't find it now. Sorry. I can replace it when I get out, if you . . ."

I knew Jasmine was wearing my cardigan.

"Hello?" Jess's head pops through the curtains, and suddenly I have two pairs of eyes on me. "Can I come in?"

"Er . . ."

"Sure, why not." Tasha sighs. "Pull up a chair."

"Oh, sorry, I don't want to intrude. I'll leave you to it."

"No, no, stay," says Tasha. "Sorry, my moods are a bit all over at the moment. I'm on a ton of morphine." Jess inches in and settles on the opposite side of the bed. "It's not as good as they say it is, but I did wake up thinking I had a lion's mane this morning."

Jess starts to giggle, and soon all three of us are smiling.

"Tasha, this is Jess," I say. "Her mom works at the library in our building."

Tasha's smile vanishes and her face drains of blood. She was pale before, but now the scratches that drag from her temple into her hairline are stark, prominent red wells in otherwise porcelain skin. "The library?" she whispers.

136

"What's wrong with the library?" I lean toward her and hesitate. Her right arm is broken, the bandages covering up a heavier plaster cast.

"It's where *he* works," Tasha whispers.

Jess sits bolt upright. "Who?"

"Him. That creepy guy I kept seeing around the drama school." Tasha's voice drips with fear and she fixes me with pupils that have retracted to tiny black dots. "Wait. You said your name was Niamh."

"Yes?" Something is crawling under my skin as she looks at me with real terror.

"I knew I remembered your name." Her voice is low now, small and quiet in the sterile room. "*Niamh.* That's what he said."

She raises a trembling finger and points it at me, and for the first time I notice her bare, bloody nail beds, where the nails have been ripped away. "The guy from the library. I could smell him. Kind of woody . . . mossy, almost." She pauses, takes a deep, gulping breath. "He followed me. He grabbed me by *your* top and whispered *your* name in my ear. Right before he attacked me."

18

"Will? He was the one who attacked you?"

I can tell Jess is trying to sound shocked, but neither of us are, not really. After getting locked in that horrible little room yesterday, it wasn't going to take much to convince us that he was the one responsible for all these attacks.

"Yeah." Tasha nods, wincing in pain. "I went into the library earlier that day and then I kept seeing him around the building." She shudders and pulls the crisp, white sheet tighter to her body before continuing. "I didn't really think anything of it, just thought he was in another course or something. But then I noticed him again, and again." She frowns with the effort of remembering. "I went to a dance class. I was walking home after, and that was when . . ."

"It's OK. You don't have to talk about it—"

"No," she interrupts me. "I do. There have been more attacks, haven't there? Since me, I mean."

"Er . . ."

"How many?"

"Two," I admit. "A girl at a station, her face was . . ." I gesture weakly to the red score lines engraved in her face. "Well, y'know. And then me, yesterday." I fill her in on the details of my own encounter and she watches me with wide eyes, barely blinking.

"The girl at the train station," Tasha says slowly. "How do you know about her face?"

"I was there." The words barely make a sound in the room, but I swear if she was a cartoon character, a big yellow light bulb would be springing out of the air above Tasha's head right now.

"So let me get this straight." Tasha uses her good hand to tick off the fingers on her bad one and I try not to grimace at the sight of her mangled nail beds. "First, you swap rooms with a girl in our course and she dies—is *murdered*—minutes later. Then you lend me your top and *I'm* attacked and put in the hospital. You go to the train station and a girl is mauled there. And finally, you're ambushed in the library where this guy, Will, works."

"Yeah," I mumble.

"Niamh, what did the other girls look like?"

"Um," I mumble again. My shoes are suddenly pretty interesting.

"They looked like you," Jess supplies quietly. "Or Niamh. Long, straight, dark brown hair, tall. I'd easily confuse them in the dark."

"Enough!" I say. "I know, I know—the victims all look

139

like me, but I'm not the link here." Jess and Tasha exchange a meaningful glance and frustration pours out of me. "I'm not! Believe what you want, but the first attack happened two weeks before I was even in the country. Check the newspapers if you don't believe me!"

"Niamh, it's OK, we believe you." Jess's voice is soothing, like she's talking to a little kid. It would usually annoy me, but I'm too tired to be annoyed. Tasha is looking exhausted, and I feel guilty.

"I'm sorry," I say. They glance at one another as I make eye contact with them both, trying to prove I'm not a total psycho.

"Don't be sorry." Tasha speaks gently. "It's not us who should be sorry."

"She's right." Jess leans over the bed, takes Tasha's free hand, and offers me her other one. I take it. A hot tear runs down my cheek. "If it is Will, we can do something about it. We'll go to the police, tell that detective everything we know. Tasha can identify him as the one who attacked her."

She squeezes my hand. "Maybe we can stop him before he does it again."

"Yeah." I squeeze her hand back, my fear slowly retreating. I look Tasha in the eyes and there's a glimmer of hope reflected there. "Yeah, maybe we can."

"I think we're going the wrong way."

"Really, you think?" Jess mutters sarcastically. She looks around at the maze of corridors. "I've never been down here before. We must've taken a wrong turn when we left Tasha's ward."

I hang back as she wanders down the passageway toward a multicolored sign. We're in a much older part of the hospital now, where the floor is chipped and dirty brown, and the lower walls are lined with that shiny green tile you sometimes see in public restrooms. I let my eyes drift along the old door frames, each one a large arch with a little Art Deco plinth on the top. The whole place is saturated with a decaying air of grandeur and sadness . . . definitely sadness.

"Back this way, I think." Jess is only a few steps away, but her voice echoes like we're at opposite ends of a cavern. I follow her, aware of how quiet it is, our footsteps falling into a steady rhythm when I catch up. "We're going straight back to the police station, right?"

"Right," I reply, distracted by the wooden plaques hung above various entrances. They're all carved with names, the gold paint faded, a ghost of its former glory. We pass the Sir Lawrence Fortescue Ward, the Lady Pembroke Neonatal Unit, the Jane Alsop Children's Unit.

"Wait." I stop dead.

"What's up?" Jess follows my gaze and her eyes clear with comprehension. "Jane Alsop, no way! She was that rich girl whose family owned the factory—the girl who died. Geoffrey told us about her."

I nod slowly. "The one I dress up as."

"I wonder why the unit was named after her. They must've been real high-society types."

"Why?"

"You had to donate a load of money to have someplace like this named after you, especially back when this was built."

"When was that?"

Jess points at the Art Deco arch I spotted earlier. "That's around 1900 or so."

"That's too late," I mutter. "Geoffrey said Jane died in 1838. This would be more than sixty years later."

Jess shrugs. "Maybe her family organized it? A remembrance thing? Better than those weird brooches we—"

I hold up one hand. "Yep, I remember. Thanks."

"Or maybe another, later relative had the same name? Or she had a memorial unit in an older building, and they kept the name when they moved to this one?"

"I guess." I feel a pinprick of, I don't know, something. I can't put my finger on it, but it seems like we got lost this way on purpose. "Jess, do you, ah . . ."

"Do I what?"

"Do you believe in ghosts?"

Jess hoots a laugh and links my arm to pull me gently onward. "Come on. We want to get to the station before Detective Moran finishes for the night."

I give myself a little shake. She's right; we need to see Detective Moran and tell him what we know. I let Jess pull me back down the corridor and over the threshold into the newer building, leaving the specters in the dark.

19

"What do you mean, Will's gone missing?" I ask. Jess hands me a cup of strong tea in a chipped mug. I check my watch; I need to be at the museum in an hour.

"He just vanished." Jess lowers her voice so that Ruth, who's hovering protectively behind the library counter, can't hear her. "I heard Mom talking to Detective Moran, and she said there's been no sign of him at all. It's like, *poof*." She makes exploding little fireworks with her fingers. "The police can't find him anywhere."

"Weird." I chew the plastic cap on the end of my pen. "Do you really think it was him who attacked Tasha?"

"I think so. You saw the marks on his hands. We know he's been in the antique books section. Yeah, it makes sense. Plus, what Tasha said about the smell—he really did smell like that. Not bad, but, like, woodsy or something. Like the tree air freshener in my dad's car." She eyes me. "Why, don't you?"

"Yeah, I guess so. I'd definitely feel better if we knew where he was."

"I think Mom would too." I can barely hear her now, her voice a wraithlike whisper. "She's been beating herself up pretty badly, said she always thought she was a pretty good judge of character."

"It's not her fault he's a total sociopath."

"No. But try telling her that."

We both watch Ruth pretending to look busy at the computer, though we know she's only there to keep an eye on us. Jess won't say anything, but I feel as though Ruth has gone off me a bit. I wonder if she's worried about me and Jess spending time together, after everything that's happened.

"Are you coming for dinner tonight?" Jess's voice is back to normal. "Dad's making his famous jerk chicken with rice and peas."

"Sounds amazing. I've been living off instant noodles for the last three days."

"I hope you can handle spice. Do you want to stay over? We can pretend to be normal, do Korean face masks and watch something cheesy on Netflix."

I hesitate for a second, before Meghan's voice in my head tells me to stop being so pigheaded and accept help once in a while. "You know what, that sounds perfect." Jess beams at me. "As long as your parents don't mind?"

"Don't be silly! Mom might actually relax if she knows you're in the next room."

"She's worried about me?"

"Of course she's worried about you!"

"Well, then, I guess I'll have to stay." The thought of being in a real house, eating a real, home-cooked meal, is the kind of excitement I need in my life right now. "Anyway, I'd better go. I'm doing the afternoon shift at the museum." I gather up the notebook I haven't used *again* and shove it in my bag. "Can we come in tomorrow so you can show me the old newspapers on the microfilm thingy? I need to do some actual research if I'm ever going to write this essay."

"Yep, no probs. We can have a lazy morning and come in later. It's always quiet on the weekend."

"Cool." I swing my bag onto my shoulder, push away from the table, and stand. "Meet you back here later?"

Jess shakes her head, her curls dancing. "No, I'll meet you at the museum."

"Jess, there's really no need. It's miles away!"

"No arguing. I don't want you on your own too much. See you at six?"

"Yeah, OK." I pause before tucking my chair in. "Thanks."

"Of course. Plus, I might finally get a sneak peek at lover boy."

"Ah, now it makes sense!" I don't blame her. I have talked about Tommy roughly every five seconds since my last shift. "Just don't embarrass me, OK?"

"As if I would."

I can still hear her laughing as the door swings shut behind me.

"Niamh, my dear, wonderful to see you." Geoffrey's voice booms over the cobblestones as I emerge into my other life. I automatically scan the room for Tommy and my heart rate speeds up as I spot him chatting to some visitors, cap in hand, his blond hair tousled and shining.

"Hi, Geoffrey." He looks a little worse for wear today, leaning heavily on his stick. I always assumed it was a prop, but maybe he actually needs it, like Ruth. "Is everything OK?"

"Oh, yes, yes—just a bit of the old gout playing up. Happens occasionally after spending the day on my feet." He removes his top hat. "I am going to call it a day, though. It's been quiet and I'm sure you and Thomas will do a grand job without me."

"Of course—don't worry about us," I blurt. Me and Tommy? Alone? In a quiet museum? "You go home and rest." Subtle, Niamh. I might as well push him out the door.

"Thank you, dear. Now," he says, wagging a finger at me, like I'm a naughty pup, "don't work too hard."

I smile. "I won't; don't you worry." He chuckles and waves his hat regally, then begins to tap toward the staff room.

"Just us two, then?" Tommy's voice teases my ear, and my insides immediately begin to melt.

"H-hey," I stutter, turning. He is smiling. "Yeah, looks like it."

"Great." He gently nudges me with his shoulder and the physical contact leaves my mind blank and my skin singing. I don't think my heart can take four whole hours of this. "So, what do you want to do, my lady?"

"Do?"

"Yeah, it's dead in here. The only visitors we've had today just left, and the weather is amazing, or so I've heard. I don't think we'll see anyone else for a while."

"Seriously?" I fall into step beside him as he meanders along the cobblestones. His hands are jammed deep into his trouser pockets, and they pull around his bottom half in a way I pretend not to notice. His hair looks soft, clean. I bet it feels amazing.

"Niamh?" Uh-oh. What did he say? He's speaking slowly, clearly repeating himself, the words coming out all slow and pronounced. "I said I have an idea."

"Er, OK."

"I'll be back in five. Meet me in the Temperance Bar?"

He's gone before I can answer.

The Temperance Bar is at the other end of the museum, in its own little corner. The lights are dimming as I start hesitantly toward it. I wish I had a flashlight or something. There's no direct route; the museum was laid out so that visitors have to walk through different shops in order to get anywhere.

I enter the apothecary, which is the start of the route to

the opposite side of the street. I pause in the shop, like I do every time I'm here. The shelves behind the scarred, wooden counter fascinate me, with rows upon rows of cloudy glass flasks and bottles. Most are empty, though some have remnants of who knows what in the bottom of them. A few even have their original handwritten labels, the ink faded and edges curled and brown. It feels like a magic shop, a far cry from a pharmacist on the high street, which is what it would have been. I could spend hours in here, but I pick up my pace again and leave through the back door into a small, cramped alleyway.

This bit, Geoffrey explained, isn't real, like the rest of the museum, but weirdly, it's always felt the creepiest to me. Above my head, white cotton tunics faintly sway on a washing line strung between two windows. There never seems to be a breeze here, so the swaying always creeps me out, like the alleyway is breathing. I think I see a long-haired figure, a swish of dark cloth out of the corner of my eye.

"Hello?" I try anyway, just in case it's a visitor who has gotten lost.

Nothing.

I open my mouth to call again but stop myself. What if it's Jasmine? Or J—

Stop it. I shiver and hurry through with my head down, passing by the tailor's and emerging into a small village square, complete with a large oak tree encircled by a wooden bench. It's nearly dark now, and an old streetlight casts a muted glow over the area.

The timeworn, mint-green facade of the Temperance Bar is partly hidden behind the tree's fake foliage. I duck around it and enter the store, inhaling the scent of cocoa that still seems to linger after all these years. I haven't really spent much time in here, so I have a good look around while I wait for Tommy.

The faded pink walls are decorated with old tin advertisements for tea and cocoa. I gather my skirts and sit down on a wooden chair at a small, round table. This reminds me so much of the little local pub back home, I get a twinge in my stomach. The smell of cocoa seems to grow stronger, and then Tommy appears in the doorway with a steaming-hot mug in each hand.

"Fancy meeting you here." He winks and puts the earthenware cups onto the table. Then he drags a stool over and sits, almost indecently close.

"Hey." Is that all I can say? *Hey?*

"Hot chocolate for the lady." He pushes a cup toward me, and the smell sets off a rumble in my stomach. I clutch my hands to it, my shoulders tense, praying he hasn't noticed, but he laughs and my muscles relax. "I hope it's all right. I couldn't find any proper stuff, so had to steal some of Sue's from the front desk's diet garbage." He holds out his mug and clinks mine, the brown liquid sloshing down the side.

I smile and clink back. "Sláinte, then." I blow on the hot chocolate as his glorious eyebrows knit together.

"Slancha?"

"Yeah, it's Irish. For cheers."

"I like it. Slancha!" He clinks my cup again and I giggle.

Ugh, God help me, I am not usually a giggler. "What you laughing at?"

"Nothing." I smile. He puts his cup back on the table and his face suddenly grows serious. He reaches a hand toward me and I hold my breath. What's he doing?

"Here, let me get that." Tommy's fingers whisper against my cheek as he brushes a single stray hair from my face. They linger there for a second and I feel like I'm going to burst into flames when he traces them down my cheek and over my jawbone. "You are so beautiful."

Is this really happening?

I close my eyes as he traces a line down the side of my neck, setting off little flurries of excitement through my body. I hear, rather than feel, my little gasp of breath when he reaches my collarbone and leans closer, pressing his warm, soft lips to the dip there. My eyes fly open and he pulls away, looking directly into my eyes.

He almost looks sad.

"Is this OK?" he murmurs, his fingers still on my neck. I nod, mainly because I've forgotten how to speak. He runs his hand gently down my arm and wraps his fingers around mine. I hold on to them for dear life as he leans toward me, our eyes meeting for a fraction of a second, before his lips finally join with my own.

20

"Why so glum, my lady?"

I jump. I didn't notice Tommy outside the museum. "Oh, it's nothing." I shove my phone into my bag. "Just a party." It's the party Jasmine mentioned the other day. Someone has put up the address on social media. Seems like everyone's going.

"A party? Cool. Where is it?"

"Oh, it doesn't matter. I'm not going." He turns me around to face him and looks at me closely.

"But you'd like to, right?"

"Well, yeah, but . . ." I sigh. "I don't really know anyone yet."

"All the more reason to go, then."

"No, really. I'm supposed to be sleeping over at Jess's. Plus, I'm exhausted. . . ." I fake a yawn and don't even get halfway through before Tommy's face crumples into laughter.

"Oh, please, you're desperate to go."

My face is starting to burn, and I try to shrug it off. "Well, it could be cool, I guess."

"You should go." He smiles and hitches his bag higher on his shoulder. He's wearing a tight black T-shirt beneath an unzipped hoodie. The shirt hem lifts and flashes me a brief glimpse of his toned, tanned stomach. A lump forms in my throat.

"Unless . . ." Should I? Would he?

"Unless what?"

There are those dimples again.

"Unless you want to come with me? Just for an hour," I venture, barely able to hear my own voice over the violent thudding in my chest.

"Where did you say it was again?" My heart slows a little. I should have known he wouldn't want to come to some stupid drama party.

"Near here, I think. Some old theater with an abandoned basement studio." Eww, even saying it out loud makes me shudder. Why do I want to go so much? Something like this is way more Meghan's scene.

"The old Regency?"

"Yeah. Do you know it?"

"Yeah. It's near here." He lowers his voice, taking a step closer and brushing my shoulders with gentle hands. "They say it's haunted."

"So I've heard," I breathe, tingles shooting out of his fingers and directly into my nerve endings. "It's not really my thing, anyway." I'd much rather stay here all night, waiting for a glimpse of that stomach again. Tommy's eyes are liquid yumminess and I blink quickly, trying not to drown in them. "Besides, there's this girl, Jasmine, who'll be there, and she loves making me miserable."

"Jasmine?"

Ugh, what did I mention her for?

"Er, yeah. She's just this girl in the course." I brush it off, but I've piqued his interest.

"And she's what? An entitled brat?" He smirks at me as I start to laugh. Talk about hitting the nail on the head.

"Pretty much," I agree, filling him in on Cardigan-gate. "She's taken a dislike to me for some reason. So there's not much point in going. I'd only be punishing myself."

"Hmm." Tommy thinks for a second. "Wait here," he says, turning back to the museum entrance. "I'll be right back."

"OK." I'm left on the street, more than a little confused. I lean back against the wall as the minutes tick slowly by and watch dark-suited office staff rushing home from work. Jess! I tap out a quick text and fill her in on the situation, and as I do, my phone pings—it's her. She's stuck at the library. There's been a leak or something, and she's on Operation Save the Books. I try not to be *too* happy about the events and let her know I'll call her after the party. After what seems like for-ever, Tommy emerges from the sliding doors, his bag looking much fuller than it did before.

"Come on, then." He holds out his hand for mine. "Let's show this Jasmine who's boss."

"Come in." A deep, theatrical voice booms up from the depths, scant flashlight flickering from the cellar. The metal rail is cool in my grip as we climb down, our feet echoing as we descend from the street into a basement.

As I arrive at the bottom, the flashlight illuminates the face of one of the guys from the course. Ben, I remember.

"Hey," I try, but my voice is swallowed by the thick, black silence. "Hey," I repeat, louder, trying to sound more self-assured. "We're here for the party?" Tommy clatters down behind me, and his presence makes me a tiny bit braver.

"Duh," Ben says, but he's smiling and beckons us to follow him. "Niamh, right?"

"Yeah. And this is Tommy."

"Cool." He nods and Tommy copies him in that weird way that boys do.

"This place is great," I say.

"I'm doing a work placement here," says Ben. "That's how I got the key."

We follow the bobbing light down a dark corridor, the beam flashing over whitewashed brick. I trail a hand along the wall and my fingers come back damp and smeared with dust. I hastily wipe the grime on my jeans. We follow in silence until Ben stops and pushes a door open, holding it with one hand as he clutches the flashlight under his chin with the other, making a face at us like we're at a five-year-old's Halloween party.

"Enter . . . but beware!" He chuckles to himself as he walks back to the entrance, the door creaking shut behind him.

I blink a few times, trying to acclimate to the darkness. It's a large studio, and everything—the floor, walls, even the ceiling—is painted black. There are a few small knots of people, some who I recognize from the course, scattered around the room, clutching cans and making hushed conversation over dozens of tea lights. The welcome warmth of Tommy's hand on my lower back reminds me that I'm not on my own and I start to sink into it, until I hear a familiar, sneering voice.

"Ugh, what is *she* doing here?" Jasmine emerges from the gloom, her hair golden and gleaming in the candlelight. Her eyes are narrow, nasty slits, but then she sees Tommy and they widen.

"Well, hi, there," she purrs in a voice I've never heard. She holds out a hand, like she's royalty or something. "Jasmine."

Jerk.

"Come on, Niamh." Tommy grabs my hand and brushes past Jasmine like he hasn't even seen her. "Let's check this place out."

I stifle my giggles as we start to explore the room, stepping around the little pockets of people cradling cans and bottles. A few people throw me a wave, but on the whole, they are gaping at Tommy.

Can't say I blame them. I straighten my posture and flick my hair behind my shoulder in a way that says, "That's right; he's with me."

"It's freezing down here," I murmur as we find a spot in a corner. Someone has thrown down some cushions, which, on closer inspection, we see are actually old, backless theater seats, their red velvet threadbare, the golden studs tarnished and dull. I thud down on one, careful to avoid the stumpy candles on the ledge behind us (I learned my lesson when Auntie Donna caught her hair on the flaming Christmas wreath last year—she still won't wear hairspray), but I regret it immediately when Tommy disappears behind a gray cloud.

"Ewww," I splutter, "dusty."

"Just a bit." Tommy drops down much more gracefully than I managed and shrugs his hoodie off as the air clears. I see Jasmine glaring at me from the other side of the room, her face petulant. "Here," he says. "Take this."

The look on Jasmine's face is just priceless. I shrug it on, relishing the warmth and the way the arms are slightly too long on me. Emboldened, I lean forward and plant a soft kiss on his cheek. "Thanks."

"No problem," he says, pulling his seat closer, his long lashes lowered. His eyes are firmly on my lips. "So," he says, leaning in, "what do you want to do?"

My eyes have barely fluttered closed when a jarring squeal of static tears through the air.

"Come on, people." Jasmine has an old microphone in hand, the cord disappearing into an ancient sound system in a tangle of wires. "This is boring. We need to do something fun."

"Spin the bottle!" a male voice shouts, and a group of guys start to snicker and nudge each other.

"I don't think so," Jasmine says with a sneer, glancing around the room. "Where's Ben?"

"Here." Ben waves. "You called?"

"This place is supposed to be haunted, right?"

He shrugs. "Apparently. There used to be an old tavern or something here before the theater. The story was that not everyone who checked in would survive the night. . . . I think the owner was knocking them off. All very Sweeney Todd."

"Perfect." She bares her straight, white teeth and presses her lips to the microphone. "Because I think we should do a séance."

"Yeah, I'm ready to go," I whisper to Tommy as the rest of the party erupts into chatter and begins to migrate toward Jasmine. My skin feels like a thousand six-legged creatures are crawling around on it. "This *really* isn't my thing."

"Oh, I don't know." Tommy pats his bag. He's grinning. "I have a trick up my sleeve. Her little séance ideas fits in almost too perfectly."

Despite my panic, curiosity stirs. "What's in there?"

"Wait and see." He stands up, brushing dust from his dark jeans. He fits in down here, all dark and brooding against the chipped black walls, the shadows setting off his strong jaw and making his cheekbones razor-sharp. He holds out a hand. "Do you trust me?"

21

"Now." Jasmine is seated at the self-appointed head of the circle, her voice low as she extends a delicate, beringed hand to either side. "Take the hand of the person next to you."

I shuffle uncomfortably, pins and needles already shooting up my legs. The cold of the floor soaks into my bones and my teeth begin to chatter. The girl next to me offers her hand and I'm about to take it when Tommy's voice echoes around the room.

"I have something better than a séance." He drags his battered old satchel in front of him and tugs at a rectangular box inside, its corners snagging on the worn leather. He eventually pulls it free and thrusts it into the circle.

Jasmine swigs from a clear glass bottle and gives him a savage grin.

"A board game? Oh, sweetie. We're not here for Monopoly."

"Take a closer look." His voice is calm. I strain my eyes

to look at the box. It's old, that's for sure, worn cardboard, sepia-toned and tattered at the edges. The bottle makes its way around and I get a whiff of something that could probably strip my nail polish, so I push my lips together, pretend to take a swig, and pass it on to Tommy. He ignores me, staring intently at Jasmine. A little knot of jealousy forms in my stomach. The skin on my lips burns.

"Fine." She sighs, leaning forward to pull the box toward her, all jangling bracelets and sparkling rings, like some kind of trust-fund fortune teller. "Oooooh . . ." She sits back, fixing her eyes on her enraptured audience. "Now we're talking."

She eases the lid from the box and I know she's aware that every single pair of eyes is on her. She flings it carelessly to the side and I cringe, knowing that if it came from the museum, it's at least a century old. She lifts out a package and slowly unwraps a small, heart-shaped piece of wood, solid except for a circle bored clear through the middle. A larger cloth-wrapped package follows, and she grunts under the unexpected weight. She places it on the floor and the material slides away, exposing a varnished wooden board.

"Oh, hell no," I hear someone mutter.

"Chicken?" Jasmine challenges. A few people start to leave the circle. "I thought so," she mocks, encouraging the remaining few to move in closer. Now that I can see what it is, I'm ready to clear out too. Then a hand on mine and a whisper in my ear changes my mind.

"I thought you trusted me," Tommy says.

"I do."

"Then watch this."

I shuffle in closer as Jasmine sits up straight, her legs crossed in some weird pretzel shape, her back straight and rigid. "I can feel the energy," she whispers.

I want to laugh at her, I really do, but the flickering candles, the basement walls, and the seeping cold convince me that it's not remotely funny.

Not to mention the Ouija board in the center of the circle.

It is marked with crudely carved letters of the alphabet, the numbers zero through nine, and the words "yes" and "no." The planchette sits in the middle of us, on top of the varnished wood.

"Everybody needs to place one finger on the planchette," Tommy instructs, and I'm surprised when everyone does it without question. There aren't many of us left in the circle now, just six—no, seven, including me. I see Ben and a couple of Jasmine's cronies. I'm so close to Jasmine that I can see her perfect eyeliner flicks.

I place my finger on the planchette. The little pointer feels charged beneath our hands and almost vibrates on the polished wood.

"Now," Tommy continues, "we need to have a common goal. The board is here to help with communication from beyond the veil. Who do you want to contact?"

Jasmine fixes me with a look so cruel, I know what she's going to say before it leaves her toxic little mouth.

"Sara Mondrial. The girl who died. I want to talk to her." She smiles. "Ask her a few questions."

Tears burn in the back of my throat. My vision starts to blur. No one makes a sound; the group seems to be holding its collective breath. I blink to clear my eyes and see that Tommy is watching me closely. He raises an eyebrow. He said to trust him—what have I got to lose? I give a little nod and he smiles.

"Good," says Tommy. "We'll try to speak to Sara. Now, we need to be clear in our questioning, all channeling the same thoughts for this to work. . . ."

"I've got this." Jasmine's eyes snap open as she cuts Tommy off. She takes a deep breath and lets it out slowly, closing her eyes once more. "Spirits," she croons, her voice low and hypnotic. "If you are with us in this room, make yourself known. Is there anybody here?"

I gasp out loud as the planchette jars beneath my finger, shooting across the board before stopping on "yes."

Jasmine clears her throat in an effort to compose herself, but I can see she's shaken, and fear ripples around the circle. Tommy catches my eye and winks. Ohhhhh.

This is his plan. Scare the bejesus out of Jasmine.

I can get on board with that.

"Thank you, spirit." Her voice is confident, but I remind myself that we're drama students. We're good at pretending. "Are you the spirit of Sara Mondrial, the tragic, beautiful victim of an untimely murder?"

I know Tommy is controlling the board—that this is all nonsense—but suddenly I can't breathe. The image of Sara's lifeless body is engraved into my memory. I close my eyes to

161

hold back the tears that are threatening to spill and feel the planchette moving again.

I peek out from beneath my lashes to see it's now resting on the word "no." Thank God. At least Tommy isn't pretending to be Sara. I shoot him a grateful glance, expecting another cheeky wink, but instead his expression is confused, his face pale.

"Can you tell us your name, spirit?" Jasmine is settling into her role nicely; all she's missing are a headscarf and a crystal ball. The pointer jerks again before gliding across the board, as though on oiled tracks. "J." Jasmine's voice wobbles slightly as she reads out the letters. "A." She looks a little green around the gills now. "N." I stare at Tommy, but his eyes are glued to the little piece of wood beneath our fingers. "E."

The planchette stops moving.

"Jane?" Jasmine whispers, and before the name is even out of her mouth, the planchette has dragged us back to "yes."

"Jane Alsop?" I whisper, and our fingers are jerked away briefly before returning to "yes."

I try to hide a smirk as I realize what Tommy is up to. I glance at him again, prepared to drop him a wink, but he is still staring at the planchette.

"Who's Jane Alsop?" Jasmine hisses, lowering her voice so only I can hear. "If you're messing with me . . . I'm warning you, you little . . ." I cut her off with what I hope is a cool stare. She does not like it when it's not all about her.

"A local girl." Tommy's voice is quiet, and I'm pretty impressed at his acting skills. I should've known he was good after seeing him lead the tours in the museum. "She died near here, in 1838."

"Jesus," the guy next to me mutters.

"Right." Jasmine switches back to her mystic persona impressively fast. "Jane," she whispers. "Why are you here? What have you got to tell us?"

The board vibrates beneath our fingers, and a hollow feeling starts to build inside me as I see what the board is spelling out.

N-I-A-M-H.

What the hell is Tommy playing at now? I glare at him, and it takes me a second to realize that the look of fear on his face is real. He catches my eye and shakes his head, confusion carved into the lines around his eyes.

If he's not controlling this, then who is?

The planchette carries on, darting around faster and faster, spelling out my name over and over again.

N-I-A-M-H.

N-I-A-M-H.

N-I-A-M-H.

"Stop!" The sound of my own voice makes the people in the circle jump and my finger loses contact with the wood, but not before my whole hand feels as though it is engulfed in flames. "I get it, you hate me, fine." I spit, pointing at Jasmine. "But this is a really messed-up thing to do."

Jasmine opens her mouth to respond, but Ben interrupts. "Er, guys?"

Six pairs of eyes shift from me back down to the board.

No one is touching it now. But the planchette is still racing around.

On its own.

I force myself to keep breathing, even though a vise of sheer horror is tightening around my chest. The marker tears around the board, returning to the same letters over and over again, repeating the pattern until it becomes a blur of varnished wood. Black spots gather at the edges of my vision as a word seems to become clear.

R-U-N-R-U-N-R-U-N-R-U-N-R-U-N-R-U-N-R-U-N-
R-U-N-R-U-N-R-U-N-R-U-N-R-U-N-R-U-N-R-U-N-
R-U-N-R-U-N-R-U-N-R-U-N-R-U-N-R-U-N-R-U-N-
R-U-N-R-U-N-R-U-N-R-U-N-R-U-N-R-U-N-R-U-N-
R-U-N-R-U-N-R-U-N-R-U-N-R-U-N-R-U-N-R-U-N-
R-U-N-R-U-N-R-U-N-R-U-N-R-U-N-R-U-N-R-U-N-
R-U-N-R-U-N-R-U-N-R-U-N-R-U-N-R-U-N-R-U-N-
R-U-N-R-U-N-R-U-N-R-U-N-R-U-N-R-U-N-R-U-N-
R-U-N-R-U-N-R-U-N

22

"Tell me everything."

It's the next morning, and Jess dumps her bag on the table between us, almost knocking my drink to the floor. We're in the café at the college, and by the sounds of it, she was in the library cleaning up with Ruth most of last evening. To wake her up, I fill her in on the horror of my night.

"I was too upset to call you," I explain. "I legged it straight to the nearest bus stop, and I haven't spoken to Tommy since."

"Do you think he was moving the board?" Jess asks. I shake my head slowly.

"At first, yeah. But he seemed as shocked as I was when it started spelling my name out."

Jess shivers. "You've given me goose bumps. That is so freaky. What do you think it was, then?"

"I really don't know." To be honest, I've been trying not to think about it. "Hey, I forgot to tell you! Last night, when I said Jane's name out loud, Jasmine said she was *warning* me."

"Warning you about what?"

"I dunno; she didn't finish."

"And she had wanted to talk to Sara's spirit?"

"Yeah." I chew on my lip. "You don't think she has something to do with it, do you?"

"I dunno. I mean, she's tiny, but then again, she's clearly got a screw loose. Look at your cardigan. She's a complete psycho."

"Yeah." I shudder, remembering the snarl distorting her face.

"Still, you went to a party with the lovely Tommy," Jess says. "That has to be a silver lining."

"I guess." I bite my lip but can't quite help the grin that spreads across my face.

"Wait." She studies me. "Did something else happen?"

"I don't know what you mean."

"It did, didn't it? Oh my God, tell me everything."

"There's not much to tell. I mean, we might have kissed, but . . ."

"Kissed?!" Jess's shriek draws amused glances from the others in the café.

"Yeah." I smile coyly. "Not much to tell, though . . ."

"Fine." She flops back in the chair across from me and shrugs. "I'm not interested, anyway. I mean, I go around making out with ridiculously hot people all the time, no biggie."

"He is *ridiculously* hot." God, my cheek muscles hurt from grinning.

Jess squeals and pulls out her phone, tracing her finger

across the screen to unlock it. "I need to see this for myself. What's his last name, again?"

"There's no point in googling him. He's a social media ghost."

"He's really not on anything? At all?"

"I don't think so."

"Weird. Does he even have a phone?"

"Of course he has a phone." As I say it, I realize I've never seen Tommy use one. But then, we're usually dressed up as Victorians, so maybe that's why. "At least, I think he does."

"Weeeeeeird. Who doesn't have a phone? He gave you his landline number though, right?"

"Err . . ."

"Niamh! Have you even spoken to him outside of the museum?"

"Of course I have! I saw him at the theater that night, remember?"

"Where you were planning to meet him?"

"No, but . . . Oh, stop it. You're kind of ruining this for me."

She folds her arms and gives me a serious look. "I'm just looking out for you. The last thing you need right now is to fall for some hot but sketchy guy who probably has a girlfriend."

My heart slides into my shoes. "You think he has a girlfriend?"

"Sorry," she shrugs. "But why else does he avoid social media? And why hasn't he given you his number? There are just a lot of red flags. Think of it this way—what would you say to your sister if she was telling you all this?"

"To be careful," I admit. I sip at my Coke. I flick my bare nails on the tab of the can, a hollow, metallic sound filling the silence. "That he probably has a girlfriend."

"Go to your workshop and forget about it. I'll see you at the library after, right?" She studies my expression. "Ah, I'm sorry, Niamh."

"Oh, it's fine." I give her a watery smile, all my excitement evaporated. "It's hardly your fault, is it? It's just . . ." I heave a sigh.

"What?"

"Nothing."

"No, go on."

I sigh again. "He's just so freaking pretty."

The library is, as usual, empty and smells of mildew and air freshener. Jess texted me to say she has an awesome idea for my scholarship essay, which is good news. I'm trying as hard as I can to think of something to write about, but I'm too exhausted and worried to think straight.

Despite what we now refer to as the "incident" last week, the library is fast becoming my safe space. There's something about Ruth's presence that's so calm and welcoming that it overshadows the bad memory.

It helps that Will isn't here any longer. There's no air of unease that followed him around. The thought of him sends a little ripple of goose bumps across my shoulders and I fight back a shudder. As much as I try not to think about him or the last few weeks, I know I won't settle properly until he's been found.

Jess is waiting at the door to a little room I haven't been in yet. "Mom gave me the idea. Come on."

It's a stark, bare space with a couple of computers on a long desk that takes up the back wall, with some other machines dotted around them. A small, narrow window high up on the wall lets in a beam of dusty light that illuminates a bank of silver filing cabinets.

"What are we doing?"

"This is where we keep the microfilm," Jess replies. She stops in front of one of the drawers. I move closer to see that all the labels have date ranges on them, each meticulously printed by hand. There's a slight squeal of metal as she pulls one open. "It starts with 1835 to 1840, tray one."

Inside there are neat rows of cardboard boxes. These are labeled too, and Jess traces a finger across the writing on each one.

"Nope," she mumbles, closing the drawer and pulling open the one underneath. She repeats the process and this time she smiles. "Here it is."

She eases the box from its resting place and replaces it with a little blue block that fits into the space perfectly. "Mom's tip. So you know exactly where to put it back."

"Clever."

She hands me the box and heads over to a computer that's

loading up programs. I drag a chair over and sit next to her. "What's in here?"

"Have a look," she instructs.

I ease the lid off the box. Inside sit little spools of film, like I imagine old-fashioned movie or newsreels to look.

"Microfilm," Jess says. "Photographs of newspapers and stuff. There are lots of old news articles on here. I was talking to Mom about your job at the museum and she recognized the name of the girl you dress up as, can you believe that?"

"Really?" I watch as Jess takes the reel from the box and starts to load it with a practiced hand. "Where from?"

"I'll show you." She starts to click the mouse and the computer screen fills with old newsprint.

She carries on clicking, newspaper pages whizzing by on the screen, before finally stopping. "Here we go. August 1838."

"That was the year Jane died."

"Yep. Mom said it was in the papers because she was from a wealthy family. Let's see . . ." Jess's brows knit behind her glasses and she scrolls through the pages. "Keep your eye out for her name."

I sigh and peer at the screen. "Jess, as interesting as this is—in a really morbid, creepy way—"

"You know me," she grins, her eyes still focused on the screen. "Morbid and creepy are my jam."

"Yeah, I do know." I still haven't forgotten the hair jewelry. "Anyway, as interesting as this is, how's it supposed to help me write this flipping essay on 'London's theatrical history'? It's due in less than a week and I still don't know where to start."

"Just wait, you'll see . . . yes! Here it is." She adjusts her glasses and sits back, reading aloud from the screen. "'After Jane's unfortunate demise, blah, blah, blah, her loving family, blah, blah, blah . . . '"

"Jess!" I say, shocked.

"Sorry, we know these bits." She continues, unfazed. "'. . . the family will make several donations in her name. These are to include a new children's wing at St. Mary's Hospital, Paddington, and a viewing gallery at the Theatre Royal, Drury Lane, where Miss Alsop spent many happy hours.'"

"No way!" I lean closer and read the article myself. "A viewing gallery—is that a box? They named one in the theater after her?"

"Yeah, that's why Mom recognized it. She used to volunteer there before her MS got bad. She said she looked up all the names of the boxes. She loves knowing the history behind stuff like that."

"Just like you."

She smiles. "Yeah, I guess so. So, do you think you can use this? For your essay, I mean."

"Maybe. I mean, I might have to visit the theater to see how to work it in." I mull it over, trying to link together the information. "It's a pretty big coincidence, isn't it?"

"What is?"

"All these links to Jane." I start to tick them off on my fingers. "First, Geoffrey thinks I look like her. . . ."

"You do."

"Yeah, fine, so first of all, I look like her. Second, we happened to get lost at the hospital and end up outside the unit her family paid for. And third . . ."

"She's going to help you write an awesome essay and win a scholarship to stay here and study drama?"

A smile creeps across my face. "Well, when you put it like that, I suppose it's meant to be, isn't it?"

23

This is so cool. Maybe one of the coolest things I've ever done.

"I can't believe your mom got us in here," I say, looking around in awe. "There's no way I'd be able to afford to come otherwise."

"Yeah, it is pretty amazing. Sorry the tickets are just for the ghost tour, though." Jess cranes her neck to look at the golden latticework that decorates the Theatre Royal, Drury Lane, and points to a series of small, curved balconies that jut out over either side of the stage. "I think Jane Alsop's box is one of those."

I nod, only half listening. I'm imagining walking out on that stage, following in the footsteps of actors spanning back hundreds of years. I can almost feel the weight of their history on my shoulders. Jess nudges me back to reality and I refocus, trailing after the small crowd who are speaking in hushed tones, their feet whispering through the plush carpet of the central aisle.

"There is, of course, a somewhat gory history on this site." The guide is beginning his tour as we catch up. He's younger than I expected, probably early twenties, wearing a leather jacket and jeans. He's well-spoken, and, despite his age, reminds me of Geoffrey. "The theater is thought to be one of the most haunted in the world and has many tales to tell." He pauses and gestures to the stage. "This building dates from 1812, though there were previously two on this site. In 1735, a famous actor named Charles Macklin killed a fellow actor in the greenroom, after an argument over a wig. Macklin himself lived to be over one hundred, but his remorseful ghost is said to walk these boards."

"What about the Gray Man?" a small American woman pipes up from in front of us.

"Ah, someone has done their research." The woman blushes and Jess rolls her eyes at me. "Yes. The Man in Gray, as he is known, is one of the more famous residents of the Theatre Royal. He is said to appear during matinees, wearing a long, gray coat and a tricornered hat." He lowers his voice and the crowd leans in; again, I'm reminded of Geoffrey and the power of a good storyteller. "During renovations in the 1840s, a skeleton wearing gray rags was discovered, buried beneath the spot where the Man in Gray's ghost is said to appear." His voice sinks to a whisper. "A skeleton with a knife through his heart."

A shudder runs down my spine as excited murmuring breaks out amongst the ghost hunters. "I'm not sure about this," I whisper to Jess as the crowd follows the guide once more.

"You're right, sorry." She looks torn. It's so much *her* thing, it's ridiculous. "I just wanted to get us in here so you could see the box."

"I know, and I appreciate it; I've just had enough creepy stuff to last a lifetime, that's all."

"Yeah, I'm sorry," Jess says, looking longingly at the tour group. We're standing by an almost invisible black door with a subtle little sign. *Backstage—No Admittance.* "Should we try to sneak off? See the box and go home?"

"Do you think we can?" I reply.

"Yeah, leave it to me."

I glance over at the guide, who has been cornered by the American lady, who is gazing up at him and aggressively twirling her hair. "He won't notice, if she has anything to say about it."

We follow the tour through the black door and wait a couple seconds for them to disappear around a bend ahead of us. Then we double back and leave.

"I don't suppose you saw the way up there?" Jess says as we step back into the theater and follow the carpeted aisle toward the entrance. Is it just my imagination, or are the lights dimmer now?

"No, I was hoping you did."

"Nope," she says with a grin. "But that's half the fun, right?"

I lift my eyebrows and shake my head at her. "How are we friends?"

"I never realized how big this place was." Jess is following behind me. "Slow down, will you?" she pants. "I'm not really an exercise person."

I laugh and wait on the landing. The boxes are right at the top of the building. We've already climbed two flights of stairs. "Ah, come on, you're fine."

She joins me and takes a deep breath. "Not *more*?"

"Yeah," I reply. "But we must be nearly there."

She groans. "No wonder Mom can't do this anymore."

"Is it really bad?" I ask as we mount what I hope is the final set of steps.

"Sometimes," Jess replies quietly. "She gets tired really quick. She couldn't handle all these steps."

"That's rough," I murmur, and Jess shrugs. I take the hint and change the subject. "Look! Is that it?"

The stairs have leveled out onto another landing, but this time there are two signs, one for *seats* and one for *boxes*. We follow the latter down a short corridor, and I scan the gold-engraved plaques that are affixed to the top of each red-velvet-curtained doorway.

Jane Alsop.

I reach a hand to the heavy curtains, and for some reason hesitate. It feels like we're a long way up. I've been in a theater box once before, when Mom got us tickets to see *Lord of the*

Dance in Dublin, and that was fine, but this place is at least twice the size.

"You OK?" Jess whispers in my ear and I jump, lost in my thoughts.

"Yeah," I whisper back, though I'm not sure why we're being so quiet. It's almost as if the building demands it. "How are you with heights?"

Jess grimaces. "Not good."

This makes me slightly braver. I was fine in my first room; this will be fine too. I feel for the edges of the curtains, my fingernails sinking into the deep, burgundy velvet as I drag them apart. They weigh more than curtains should, as if they're filled with the hushed whispers of the theater or have soaked up the secrets of decades of visitors. Visitors like Jane.

"Wow," I breathe as I step inside. The interior is opulent. Gold brocade fabric lines the rounded walls. The seats have worn, curving arms that reach around, almost as if waiting to embrace their occupants. I edge into the box, staying well behind the seats—the balcony railing is far too flimsy-looking for my liking—and gaze down into the stalls below. A twinge radiates from my feet and up my legs; seems it's a bit different when there's no wall to stop me from falling to my death.

"Nope, I can't do it." Jess hovers by the entrance, her shadow still outside the doorway. "It's making me dizzy already. I'll wait out here." The curtains fall shut, blocking out the light from the corridor and the modern day with it.

I close my eyes, trying to imagine that I'm wearing my

museum costume. How many times did Jane visit this theater? Did she watch performances from this very box, or did she sit somewhere else? Am I looking at the stage from the same perspective she did? I open my eyes slowly, trying to see what she would have seen. I wonder if she longed to act too. To be on the stage, rather than looking down at it.

A figure in the stalls catches my eye.

It must be the tour group. I drop down behind the chairs so they can't see me, my breath coming in little gasps.

"Jess," I hiss. "Jess!" No response. The curtain is too thick, designed to keep the noise from the corridor out. I wait, then slowly unfold myself into a standing position, relying on the heavy shadows of the curtain to hide me. I glance at the seats below and freeze.

It's not the group after all. It's one solitary figure. One solitary figure, dressed in gray.

24

"Niamh! Niamh, what's happening?"

Light pours in through the curtains as Jess rips them apart. I instinctively cover my eyes as it burns into my retinas.

"Niamh!" She crouches next to me and wraps her fingers around my wrists, prying my own hands from my face. They're wet with tears. I look up at her, confused, and it takes me a second to realize I've screamed.

"There . . . there was a . . ." Sobs clog my throat, and I can't get the words out. I point over the chair and Jess turns, uneasy. "I saw something. Or someone."

She pulls me gently to my feet. "This is all my fault, I'm sorry."

"Wh-what do y-you mean?" I stop and take a deep, shaking breath, leaning on the box wall, my eyes firmly shut.

"I mean, I shouldn't have brought you on a stupid ghost tour! What was I thinking?"

"It's fine." I concentrate on sucking air deep into my lungs. "Is he still there?"

"What?"

"The gray man. Is he still there?"

"What are you talking about? Niamh, open your eyes."

I part my wet eyelashes just enough to see into the stalls of the theater.

Empty. The theater is empty.

MegaMegs2004:
A PROPER ghost?

It's_pronounced_NEVE:
YEP

MegaMegs2004:
Are u sure??!

It's_pronounced_NEVE:
. . . .

MegaMegs2004:
Are you losing it?

It's_pronounced_NEVE:
No!

It's_pronounced_NEVE:
I don't think so . . .

MegaMegs2004:
You wanna FaceTime?

It's_pronounced_NEVE:
No. I look like a dog's dinner.

MegaMegs2004:
Call, then? Need to talk to you.

It's_pronounced_NEVE:
???

It's_pronounced_NEVE:
Sure, gimme 5 xx

MegaMegs2004:
xx

I unplug my phone from the charger and shut down my laptop, moving myself from the desk to a comfier position on the bed. I don't think I've ever been this tired—unsurprisingly, I'm still finding it hard to sleep. The phone begins to vibrate—Meghan is calling.

"Hi." The sound of her voice usually raises my spirits, but she sounds oddly flat.

"What's up?" I ask.

"Mom wanted to call you but she's busy so I said I'd do it."

"Okaaay . . ."

"She said to tell you not to worry."

"About what? Why would I worry?"

"Granny's in the hospital."

"Oh." Not again.

"Yeah."

"Is it the cancer?"

"They're not sure." A faint crackle on the line is the only sound for a few seconds until Meghan clears her throat. "Mom stopped by this morning and found her at the bottom of the stairs. She'd fallen. She's broken her arm." Her voice catches, thick with sobs. "And her face is all bruised. I heard Mom telling Daddy that there was loads of blood from where she'd hit her head."

"Poor Granny! How is she feeling?"

Meghan mumbles.

"Say that again? I can't hear you."

"She hasn't woken up yet."

I don't stay on the phone for long after that. I can hear how upset Megs is. She didn't exactly tell me to come home, but I know she wants me there.

I get into bed and stare at the ceiling in the dark. Pull my sheets up so just my face is visible, burrowing down into the duvet. I can't go home now. Knowing Granny, she would never forgive me if I went back and she was OK. She's a stubborn old bird and the one who encouraged me to follow a dream she never got the chance to.

On the other hand, she's not well and she's my granny.

I wish I could sleep on it.

Hours pass. Eventually, I flick my phone on to see that it's almost three in the morning. There's no way I'm going to sleep feeling like this, so I do what Granny would tell me to do: not lie here fretting, but go and make something warm to drink, so I climb out of bed to venture to the kitchen.

The air has a bite to it as I close the door gently behind me and start to pad down the hall, grateful for my thick pjs and heavy socks. Hardly glamorous, but I'm way past caring. I wrap my hand around the little packet of hot chocolate burrowed deep into my wide pockets and pray that no one has stolen my milk again.

I remember the last time I walked down the hall in the middle of the night and feel a shiver of unease, but the elevator is quiet and the lights are on. I'm on the first floor now, directly above reception, and I'm insanely grateful for that.

My milk is in the fridge, safe and sound, and I ease open cupboard doors in search of a small saucepan. I find one, a dull silver thing that needs a good wash, and start to run the hot tap.

My thoughts are miles away as I scrub the pan—back at home, with Granny. I dry it on a questionable-looking towel and turn on the cooktop, which is splattered with what I hope is Bolognese sauce. The familiar ritual soothes me: pouring the milk, letting it bubble up into foam, and adding three hefty scoops of powdered chocolate, before whisking it all together with a clean fork. I let it boil a few seconds longer and then take it off the heat, giving it a little time to cool down.

I wander over to the large corkboard and stare blankly at old notices advertising tutors and university nights out. There are long windows in the kitchen and the streetlights outside are bright. Bright enough that I didn't have to turn the light on when I came in.

Which means I see the figure outside before he sees me.

Will.

My breath hitches painfully as I drop to the floor for the second time that day. I pull my phone from my pocket and inch up carefully, snapping a few pictures, even though I know they'll be too grainy and dark to show anything. It's definitely him, though, watching the building. Watching me? The curve of his nose is unmistakable, and I can see his long hair from here. I could swear he's wearing a gray jacket too. Was it Will who I saw at the theater? Has he been following me, like he followed Tasha? I glance down at my phone and hesitate. It's three in the morning. I'll wake Detective Moran if I call him now.

Well, it's that or go back to bed and wait to be murdered.

I dial the emergency number.

"Hello?" A male voice, thick with sleep, answers on the third ring. "Detective Moran speaking."

"Hi," I whisper urgently, my voice low, even though I know Will can't hear me through the window. "Sorry, I didn't want to wake you. . . ."

"Miss Hughes?"

"Yeah, erm. He's here."

"What?" Detective Moran's voice sharpens and I can hear rustling. I imagine him sitting up in bed.

"Will. He's here. At my dorm. Well, not here, but he's outside. I can see him from the kitchen." The other end of the line is quiet.

"OK," he replies. "Listen carefully. I'm on my way. Is he still outside?"

I risk a quick look. "Yeah."

"Right. I want you to go back to your room and lock the door. I'm going to stay on the phone till you're in your room, and radio for a police car to be there as soon as possible. Keep your lights off, and, whatever you do, do not open the door until you hear it's me. OK?"

"OK." I barely hear my response over the blood rushing in my ears. Adrenaline kicks into overdrive as I crawl to the door and run back down the corridor and into my room. I try to shut the door carefully, quietly, and turn the lock before leaning against it. I've never realized how flimsy it is.

"Miss Hughes?" Moran's tinny voice rattles from the speaker and I raise the handset to my ear. "Are you back in your room?"

"Yes," I breathe.

"Good. Help is on the way. I'm not far, but the team will probably arrive before I do. I still want you to stay put until I get there, no matter what you hear, do you understand?"

"Yes," I repeat, my voice small.

"Now, barricade the door if you can and stay away from it." I push myself off the wood as though it has burned me. "I'm going to hang up the phone, and I want you to keep the line clear until I call again. Can you do that for me?"

I nod, even though I'm fully aware he can't see me.

"I'll be there in a couple of minutes, Niamh. Sit tight for me."

The line goes dead.

I need to barricade the door. I look wildly around the room. The desk is fixed to the floor and the wardrobe to the wall—there's no way I'm budging either of those. The bed is bolted down too. My desk chair is the only thing I can move, and I grab it, racing back to the door to wedge it under the doorknob, like I've seen in a hundred horror films. I always wondered what it would do, and the answer suddenly becomes painfully clear.

Nothing. It will do nothing.

I curl up on my bed, wrapping myself into a tight little ball, as far from the door as I can get. I'm starting to wish I'd brought the pan from the kitchen; a pathetic weapon would surely be better than no weapon at all. There's a plastic coat hanger on the carpet, so I reach out and pick it up, brandishing it in front of me. I watch as the minutes crawl by on my phone screen. Three . . . four . . .

The door handle rattles.

My heart stops as I watch it turn, slowly, slowly. It stops for a few seconds and I wonder if I've imagined it, but then I hear a scraping, a scratching sound, as though someone is sliding a key in from the other side.

The handle starts to turn again, and a loud click fills the room.

The door begins to open.

No, no, no, no, no. Dear God, please don't let this be real. I'll do anything, anything you want, anything, if you just help me. . . .

The doorknob catches on the top rung of the chair and stops.

Holy hell. It does work.

I glance around wildly, looking for my key ring. It's on top of my bag. My thoughts flash back to something Daddy always does at home; he leaves the key in the lock. He says no one can get in even if they have a copy.

The chair begins to slide with a sickening scrape and I know I only have seconds, so I launch myself across the room, scoop it up, and throw my full weight at the door, slamming into the chair as I do so. Pain explodes in my hip, tiny fireworks erupting behind my eyes, but I grit my teeth and focus on the doorknob, jamming the key in and twisting it. There's a faint, metallic noise of something falling to the floor on the other side and I back away, praying my key stays in the lock.

Silence on the other side, but the blood roaring in my ears is deafening. I'm frozen to the spot, scared to do so much as breathe.

Is he still out there?

I suck in a great gulp of air as blue-and-red lights wash over the walls. I peer out my window, down to the parking lot below, where two patrol cars pull in wildly. Uniformed officers jump out, handcuffs at the ready, leaving the car doors wide open.

Footsteps thump on the stairs.

"Niamh." Never before has the sound of my own name made me want to cry. The voice seeps in through the cracks in the wood and buries itself deep under my skin. "Niamh," it breathes.

"Leave me alone!" I scream at the door and release all the anger and fear I've been carrying around. "Just leave me alone, you—you creep!" I run to the door and pound on it, battering it until my knuckles are bruised.

"Niamh, Niamh!" Another voice breaks through my rage.

"Who is it?" I stutter, stupidly.

"Answer your phone!"

I look over to my bed, where the screen is flashing in the darkness. Detective Moran.

I pick up the phone with shaking hands. "Hello?"

"We've got him, Niamh. We've got him. Stay put. . . ."

Too late. I twist my key and wrench the door open. Detective Moran is in the hall, on his phone, while two uniformed officers straddle a gaunt, lanky figure in gray behind him.

25

"How you doin'?" Derek places a steaming cup of hot chocolate in front of me on the reception counter, where I'm perched on his stool. "Moran said you were making this when you saw that creep out the window. Thought you'd appreciate it now. Calm you down."

I glance up at him gratefully. "You know it's OK that you didn't see him outside, right? It's not your fault."

"Yeah, but it is my job." He pushes the cup closer and I take the hint.

"Thanks," I croak. "Making a habit out of this, aren't we?"

Derek smiles grimly. "I reckon that's it done now, Irish."

I let the silver foil blanket around my shoulders fall as I clutch the mug with both hands, letting the heat seep into my bones. "Do you really think so?"

"Yeah." He sits down next to me and we both watch the sky growing lighter beyond the foyer's glass doors. "They've got the scumbag. You can get on with your life."

"Not like Sara," I whisper.

"No." Derek's shoulders slump. "Not like Sara. I couldn't save her."

"Niamh! Oh my God, are you OK?"

Jess practically jumps me as I walk into the library, closely followed by Ruth, who rubs my arm gently. Jess clings to me like a snail.

"I'm fine," I pant. "Jess, you're squashing me."

"Sorry!" She lets go, looking sheepish. "I'm just so glad you're OK. Come on, tell me everything."

"Jess . . ." Ruth's voice holds a warning note.

"It's fine, honestly." I sigh. "We know what she's like, right?"

"Unfortunately," Ruth replies dryly, and I laugh as Jess rolls her eyes. "I'm glad you're all right too, dear." Ruth gives me a much gentler hug. "I'm sorry I exposed you to him."

"Don't you dare, Mom." Jess's voice holds the warning now. "You couldn't have known he was a total psycho. Besides, you didn't employ him; the school did."

"Yes, I know, I know." Ruth sighs and it's clear this isn't the first time they've had this conversation. "Go on, then, you two—go catch up. Are you at the museum later today, Niamh?" I nod. "And have you called your parents?"

I nod again, but I feel uncomfortable. I did text Megs to say they'd arrested Will, but that was all. My parents have enough to worry about.

Ruth smiles. "Good. Let's all go somewhere nice for dinner, shall we? Jess, you pick—just not that Indian place we went to last time. My taste buds have only just grown back." Jess rolls her eyes as Ruth walks back to the counter, and I notice she isn't using her cane today. "See you both later."

"Bye," we echo, walking out the door. The university is quiet this early—no lectures or anything going on. I only came in to catch Jess up on last night.

"All right," she says as we settle into the comfy chairs by the cafeteria window. "Tell me everything."

Jess refuses to let me go anywhere on my own after I tell her about my dramatic night, so she ends up walking across town to the museum with me. As much as I appreciate the company, I'm pretty sure she just wants to catch a glimpse of Tommy. We arrive and relief floods over me—along with the cool air of the basement building—when I manage to leave her at the door.

"Ah, Niamh. How lovely to see you." Geoffrey's comforting baritone echoes across the foyer. He's at the front desk in his normal street clothes—"civvies," he calls them—and the effect is strangely unsettling. He just doesn't look like himself without a freshly starched collar and top hat.

"Hey, Geoffrey. You not performing today?"

"Unfortunately, not." He leans back in his chair and narrows his eyes at me. "Is everything OK? You look tired. Not working too hard, I hope."

"Just burning the candle at both ends," I fib. I'm glad he

191

doesn't seem to know what's going on. At least here I can pretend to be normal.

"You need to look after yourself, young lady. All that gallivanting won't do you any good." There is concern in his voice and I feel my cheeks warm. I feel bad for lying to him. "Oh, how could I forget!" He retrieves a thin volume from beneath the desk and slides it over to me. "I had this at home, a bit of theatrical history for your research. I once acted too, you know."

"You did? Thank you." I lift the book gently, sensing it's important to him. "I'll look after it and bring it back as soon as I'm finished with it."

"Of course you will; I don't doubt that. Anyhow, you best run along. Sue rang in sick, so I'm manning the front desk. You'll need to go and help young Thomas today. I have a feeling it may be a busy shift."

I nod and push through the turnstile when he presses down the button to let me in. First Will is arrested and then I find out it's just me and Tommy, again. Is that a good thing? I remember my conversation with Jess, but once I think about the feeling of Tommy's lips on mine, excitement begins to mingle with the doubt.

Maybe things are starting to look up after all.

Or maybe not.

As my luck has it, I've seen Tommy a grand total of three times today, each time no longer than a quick nod and a wave.

I wonder whether he's avoiding me, but I think that's paranoia; I've been run off my feet and he has been too.

Geoffrey was right; it was the busiest shift I've ever worked, but for the first time, I forgot about everything outside these walls. I'd forgotten how much I love the rush of performing for a crowd, and it almost felt like I could really be Jane Alsop. Eventually I finish up, curtsy to the final tour group, and head to the staff room. As soon as I sit down, I realize my feet are killing me. I ease off my ballet flats, vowing to wear sneakers from now on, no matter what it looks like, and start to rub the arch of my foot, letting out a low moan.

"Hey."

Tommy's deep voice and silhouette fill the staff room doorway. He joins me on the wooden bench and I quickly shove my feet back into my flats, hoping they don't stink.

"Hey, yourself," I reply. I don't know what else to say, so we sit in silence, our shoulders millimeters away from each other. I swear there are sparks crackling in the space between us. "Busy shift," I try.

"Yeah." He gives me that grin, the one that pushes a dimple into his cheek. "So, this is kind of awkward, yeah?"

I grin back; I can't help it. "Just a bit." He nudges me with his electric shoulder and the current zaps around my body, to places that just thinking about make me blush. He holds out a hand, palm up, and beckons to mine with curled fingers. I hold my breath and slide my hand into his, nervous because I know mine is clammy and hot. His fingers are cool and firm in contrast, like stones that have been washed smooth by an endless tide. There's something soothing about them.

"What are you doing now?" he murmurs. I look up at the clock and see it's already ten past six. Damn it.

"I'm meeting my friend and her parents for dinner, at eight," I say, an apologetic note in my voice. "Some Greek place near the Tower of London."

"Nice." He looks at me thoughtfully. "I would like to show you something first, though, if you have time?"

"Really?" I look at the clock. "Yeah, I think I do. It's not that far to Tower Bridge, is it?"

"Not really." He smiles. "And then I can walk you to meet them."

"That would be perfect." I grin back. Will might be in custody, but the thought of walking alone still isn't the most appealing. Plus, if he walks me to the restaurant, Jess might finally get her glimpse of him. "I'd like that, but only if it's not out of your way."

He stops pacing and smiles down at me. "Not at all—I'm staying out that way. Near Potter's Field."

He's still vague about where he lives. I try not to think about what Jess said, that he might have a girlfriend somewhere.

But I can't think about that right now, not when he's standing there, looking so, so hot.

"OK, then, great!" We grin at each other before I realize we're still wearing our costumes. I stand up and start to twist the combination into my padlock. "We need to get changed, though. See you upstairs in five?"

"Yeah, see you there."

After he leaves, I pull the dress over my head and throw on the strappy sundress I'd optimistically packed that morning, trying to push the creases out with my hands. Mom would be furious if I left the house without my dress being freshly ironed, but I don't have time to worry about it.

I grab my things and run to the mirror, quickly unwinding my hair from its braid and shaking out the waves with my fingers. I pull out my makeup bag and top up the concealer beneath my eyes, give myself a liberal dusting of bronzer to stop myself from looking like a total zombie, and then finish off with a slick of mascara. A quick roll of deodorant and a blast of body spray gets me feeling as fresh as possible after six hours in that costume, and fast as I can, I'm out the door.

I emerge from the museum into the street and see that I've beaten Tommy there. Perfect. Now that I'm back aboveground, I grab my phone and fire off a quick message to Jess: *On way to a mystery date location with Tommy! Then he's walking me to dinner. Be outside for a peek at the hottie at eight xx*

"Hey." I press the lock button on my phone before Tommy can see the text and try to act casual.

"Oh, hi, that was fast," I babble. I throw my phone into my bag. We start to walk and I can smell something sweet. "What's that smell?"

"Caramelized nuts. To tide you over till dinner. Want

one?" He offers me a little paper bag and I realize we're walking past a street cart selling them. He must've bought them while I was still inside.

"Er, yeah, OK." I take one gingerly. It's warm and sticky between my fingers, but when it hits my tongue, it melts in a little explosion of salty sweetness.

"Good?"

"Amazing!" I say, just as my stomach rumbles loud enough for the whole street to hear. Tommy looks shocked for a second and then roars with laughter, pushing the bag into my hands.

"Here, you must be starving." I try to hand them back, mortified, but he pushes them away. "Please, I insist. London delicacy."

We continue in silence as I munch on the salty little treats while trying not to eat them all in one go. We walk along the riverbank and I point to a lone person walking on the foreshore, eyes focused on the ground. He stops every few inches to crouch down and scan the sand, picking objects up and stowing them away carefully. "What's that guy up to?"

"He's mud larking," Tommy replies, pausing to glance over the wall.

"What now-ing?"

He grins at me and my eyes skim across the curve of his jaw and travel down to his unbuttoned collar. He's still wearing the white shirt from his costume. It is tight in all the right places and suddenly very distracting.

"Mud larking. When people go and look for bits of treasure along the Thames."

I eye the gray expanse of water skeptically. "Treasure?"

"That's what Geoff would call it. He's got a license for mud larking, you know."

"Why does that not surprise me?"

I polish off the nuts, crumpling the bag in my hand as we set off walking again. I drop the garbage in a nearby trash can and glance at my phone. No response from Jess. It's half past six already.

"Who's that in the photo?" Tommy asks, nodding at my phone.

"That's my little sister. Meghan." I hold it up for him to see. Her sweet, pretty, freckled face beams out of my phone, ringlets of dark brown hair tumbling about her shoulders.

"She looks just like you. Is she in Ireland?"

"Yeah, she's only a year younger than me. We were going to try and persuade my parents to let her visit, but after everything . . ." I trail off, realizing that I haven't told Tommy anything about Will, only the attacks over the last few weeks. I can't face ruining our romantic walk with the story. "After everything with my granny," I correct myself, "it doesn't look like she's going to come."

"You wanna talk about it?" Tommy asks gently.

"No, it's fine. I'm just not sure what to do. . . ."

He's so easy to talk to and I feel so comfortable with him. Granny's medical history and my doubts about staying in

London pour out of me. I even start to tell him about the scholarship and how much I'd love to stay. Is it just me, or did his face brighten a little when I mentioned that? At some point during my monologue, Tommy wraps a hand around mine and I finally stop.

"Sorry. I'm babbling."

"Not at all. Listen. I think it would be great if you stayed." We lock eyes for a few seconds and the strength of the tug in my chest starts to scare me.

He points at a large, soaring sign that declares us to be at Borough Market. "We're here."

26

We head into the market. There are no stalls yet, just pavement, but I can see visitors heading toward a covered area. I try my best not to glance up at Tommy too often, but I can't help it; my eyes keep pinging back up to the gorgeous curve of his mouth. It's twisted slightly, but in a nice way. Amused.

Oh, God—it's because I'm staring. I'm forcing myself to look ahead as he politely pretends not to notice that I'm acting like an absolute weirdo, when my body lurches forward and the pavement rushes up to slap me in the face.

"Whoa, there!"

I thrust out my hands to break the fall, but Tommy's there first, sweeping me up like I'm some 1950s starlet. I should right myself, but instead I soak up the heat radiating from his body into mine.

He smiles down at me and brushes a stray lock of hair behind my ear, his fingers tracing a soft line down to my chin. He gently places me back on my feet and gestures to a loose paving slab.

"Careful." His mouth does that twisty thing again and my insides turn to mush. "You should really watch where you're going."

"Thanks," I manage. We turn a corner, and his eyes light up.

"What do you think?"

I've been to plenty of markets at home before, like the cattle mart my granddaddy used to drag us to as kids, but they were full of old men and stank of cows. This is classy in comparison. Food stalls come into view, piled high with artfully arranged bread, cheese, and cured meat. A trio of women slide past us, swinging designer bags in the crooks of their elbows, expensive sunglasses perched on immaculate blowouts.

"It's pretty cool," I say. "Do you come here a lot?"

"I've been coming here since I was a boy. It's changed a lot since then." A jolt of electricity races up my fingers and I look down to see his hand brushing mine. "Is this OK?"

I nod, not quite able to manage words. He slides his fingers through mine, lacing them together. They interlock as though they were made to do it.

"Come on." He pulls me along gently, pointing out the original features of the market as we weave through the crowds. I do try to listen to him, but my inner self is too busy squealing with joy and mentally high-fiving strangers.

"See this?" Tommy slows to a stop and points up at a

small blue plaque, so I give myself a little shake and refocus. "Geoffrey was part of the campaign to get it up there."

" 'London's oldest fruit and veg market,' " I read aloud. "Huh, cool. He's into everything, isn't he?"

"Yeah, he loves his history. I think his father used to work here when he was a kid."

"Father, very formal," I laugh, and it is finally Tommy's turn to flush red.

"Dad, then." He tugs on my hand as I laugh and draws me closer to him, burying his face in my hair. "Are you making fun of me, Miss Hughes?"

"Maybe." I close my eyes as his warm breath tickles my ear, my body relaxing as his free arm wraps around my waist.

He plants a chaste kiss on my forehead, his lips soft, gentle on my skin. "I wanted to show you something."

"OK." I float behind him, trying to pay attention to the historical facts he shares. We pass a million food stalls that I desperately ignore, dinner only over the horizon. I listen to Tommy instead—he joked that Geoffrey was into his history, but he's not too shabby himself.

"So this place is a thousand years old? Jeez."

"Kind of." He pushes his sandy hair back from his fore-head, craning his neck to look at the green steel beams that arch over our heads. "Some of it. The original site was on the other side of the river. This one has been here since the sixteen hundreds. The building is all Victorian, though."

"It's pretty." It is. Ornate columns stretch up to a flourish beneath the glass sky above us. There isn't a cloud, just clear blue, as far as the eye can see.

"Here." A floral scent alerts me to where we are before I look back to Tommy. Sure enough, we're somehow standing in a little oasis. All around him, flowers spill from silver buckets and hanging baskets and greenery bursts from pots of all shapes and sizes, each one perched on a series of apple crates, set on their sides to form shelves.

"What do you think?"

"Oh." His hand slides from mine as I wander farther into the thicket of flowers. "It's beautiful."

Tommy beams at me.

"I thought you'd like it."

I walk deeper into the stall, ducking through the curtain of foliage and into another little world. My fingers reach out to dance along petals of their own accord and a soft, velvet scent tickles my nose. Brief chatter invades the little haven as Tommy follows me through the fronds, dropping them back and blocking out the world once more.

"China roses." He eases a flower from the tall steel pot and tucks it behind my ear. Oh. My. God. Wait until Meghan hears about this.

I point to a lily. "These are pretty too."

I try to keep my voice light, but it comes out husky and I clear my throat, embarrassed that he has such an effect on me. Embarrassed, but delighted too. The lilies remind me of my granny's house—well, how it used to be, before she got sick.

The petals are splayed out proudly, their white edges bleeding into dark pink centers.

Tommy shakes his head, frowning. "Not lilies. They're death flowers."

"Are they?" I ask. "I didn't know that."

Tommy smiles faintly. "My moth—mom—taught me about flowers. You know flowers used to have their own kind of secret language? Floriography, it was called." He traces an idle finger along a rope of ivy. "People would send tussie-mussies to one another in the Victorian times."

"Tussie-mussies?" I laugh—it sounds even more ridiculous when I say it.

"Yeah, it means 'talking bouquets.' The flowers in the bouquet would each have a special meaning for the recipient. Like a secret language."

"That's kind of cool." I try to sound casual, sensing my chance to learn a little bit more about him. "Do you live with her? Your mom, I mean."

"No." His voice is low, and a current of sadness runs below it. "She died when I was younger."

"Oh, God, Tommy. I'm so sorry. . . ."

"It's fine." He waves the apology off and takes hold of my fingers again, loosely. "It was years ago."

"That must have been so hard for you."

"Yeah." His eyes glaze over, as he's lost to a memory. "I miss her."

"I'll bet."

Silence lingers between us, but it's not awkward. It's comforting, like sharing a secret with an old friend. For a second, I could swear I've known him forever.

"Come on, then," I say. "I want to hear more about this secret language of flowers. What about this?"

I pick up a bundle of small purple flowers, tied with brown string, and revel in the calming smell. Lavender.

"No, not good, either." He laughs, back to his old self. "Lavender means caution, mistrust. You're really bad at this, you know."

"You'd better teach me, then." I begin to drag him around the little stall, pointing out flowers for him to decode. He stops in his tracks and pulls me back toward him.

"There's a reason I chose the China rose for you." He reaches up and lightly brushes the petals in my hair. I hold my breath to stop it from coming out in little gasps, my stomach tensing. "Don't you want to know why?"

"Why?" I manage.

"It means you're beautiful," he whispers, sending ripples across my skin, "just the way you are. Your eyes, these freckles . . ." Light fingers cup either side of my face and he strokes gentle thumbs from my nose across my cheeks to my hair, which he wraps around his fingers and tugs gently. "Your beautiful hair." He fixes his gaze on my mouth and I swear I'm going to lose it as he leans toward me, his face almost touching mine. "Your lips," he whispers.

I'm pretty sure there are fireworks going off somewhere when he touches his lips to mine. My body responds immediately, hungrily leaning into every part of him I possibly can. Little stars dance behind my eyes and I feel dizzy, light-headed, I . . .

"Can I help you?"

I crash back to Earth as the voice breaks us apart. A small woman in a starched apron is eyeing us with amusement and I try to look everywhere but her face.

"Yes, please," Tommy says smoothly. "I'd like to buy this beautiful girl some flowers."

I don't know if I want the ground to swallow me whole or if I should tap-dance on it. The woman smiles indulgently.

"I've got just the thing." She nods toward the flower in my hair. "You'll be taking that one too, I assume?"

"Of course." Tommy winks at me and I giggle. Seriously, who am I?

"I think this would be perfect." She holds out a tiny bunch of pink flowers that are attached to a pure-white ribbon. "It's a corsage. They're normally worn to dances and weddings and such, but this seems like a special occasion."

"It is." Tommy smiles at me and I almost split my lip grinning back. "What are they?"

"Rhododendrons." The florist gestures for me to hold out my wrist and wraps the ribbon around it once, twice, three times, finishing it off with a bow. They're beautiful, like a perfect little hybrid of a lily and the China rose in my hair.

"Thank you." I glance at Tommy, surprised to see that his face is set, serious. "What do these mean? Something good, I hope."

"Oh, Niamh, you have no idea." He smiles as he pulls out his wallet and pays with cash. I hold my hand out to admire the corsage while he waits for his change. We thank the florist, and, feeling bold, I take Tommy's hand and stand on tiptoes to plant a kiss on his cheek.

"Thank you. That was perfect."

He wraps both arms around my waist and drops a light kiss onto my lips. "No, Niamh. *You're* perfect."

As reluctant as I am to leave Tommy, it's nearly eight. I'm desperate to tell Jess everything, so I fire off a text, letting her know I'll be there soon. I chatter away about Meghan and my family back home, until I realize we've left the bright lights of the South Bank behind. We're walking along a much quieter backstreet now.

"Where are we?"

"I wanted to show you one more thing." We carry on walking, and a tickle of unease crawls down my back. It's creepy here, an unfamiliar area, and suddenly Tommy looks just like what he actually is—a guy I barely know. I drop his hand casually and reach for my phone. Still no response from Jess.

"I don't think I have time, sorry—I don't want to be late. Another time?"

"Yeah, of course."

He smiles, but I feel as though something has changed. We walk on for a while in silence, passing a large, rambling graveyard as I spy the lights of Tower Bridge in the distance. Gradually the streets become busier and the knot of tension in my chest dissolves.

I take Tommy's hand again, and feel his fingers squeeze mine.

27

"So, will I see you at the museum next week?" Tommy asks.

"No. You will tomorrow, though. It's my last shift."

"I didn't know." His face softens and he looks disappointed. "But you might be staying, right? If you get this scholarship money?"

"Yeah, but it's a pretty slim chance. The last day to hand in the application is Monday and I've barely started, and—"

He raises an eyebrow. "It sounds to me like you're looking for excuses."

I start to argue, but my mouth stays hanging open like a shocked goldfish. He's right. Everything that has happened— with Will, with Sara and Tasha, with Granny—has left me unsure. "I guess I am."

"So go for it. Send it in. What's meant to be will be and all that."

"OK." I smile. He wants me to stay! My hormones are doing a little jig at the thought.

"Fingers crossed, then." He gently tugs me closer to him, and lowers his head to mine, brushing a kiss on my cheek. "I really don't want to lose you. Not again."

"There you are!" A familiar voice interrupts and Jess appears like an overexcited jack-in-the-box. "I was waiting for you—Mom and Dad have already gone in. But I see you're busy. . . ."

Tommy and I break apart, flustered.

"Ohhhh." She draws the word out, looking at him way more intensely than seems appropriate. "Hi."

"Jess?" I mutter through gritted teeth. She blinks, as though pulled from a daze, and looks back at me. "Jess," I repeat, "this is Tommy. From the museum."

"Hi," she replies smoothly, though she's clearly giving him the once-over. "Tommy. I've heard so much—" I clear my throat. "I mean, almost nothing, about you."

Smooth, Jess.

"Nice to meet you too," Tommy says politely. "Um, I'll see you tomorrow, then, Niamh."

"Yeah, tomorrow." It's almost painful to watch him disappear back into the lucky crowds of tourists who get to swallow him up and carry him away. I wait until he's out of sight and then turn to Jess, who's still staring after him.

"Earth to Jess!" I tease. "What the hell was that back there? You stared at him like he was an alien or something."

"Sorry." She is frowning. "I just . . . I dunno. I feel like I recognize him from somewhere."

I feel like she's not telling me the full story, but with perfect timing, my stomach audibly growls.

"Hungry?"

"Always. Come on, you weirdo." I link an arm through hers and we walk toward the restaurant. "Let's go and celebrate these horrible few weeks finally being over—and the fact I'm about to pull an all-nighter to win this freaking scholarship."

I'm back in the streets behind the South Bank again, the graveyard looming out of the low fog in front of me. Weird—I've only ever seen fog like this on the fields at home, never here in the city. I try to walk away, but something irresistible pulls me forward, a tug that my feet can't deny.

Huge, wrought iron gates rise up out of the ground in front of me. They're open, parted just enough for me to slip through, so I do, walking a path I didn't realize I knew. Crooked headstones erupt out of the impenetrable, cotton fog and a stone angel, its carved eyes hollow and blank, peers at me through the gloom. I'm strangely calm as I walk deeper into the cemetery, until I pause in front of a small building, my feet now fused to the ground.

It's a mausoleum.

I can't remember ever seeing one of these before, but I know instantly what it is. I seem to float around to the front, where an arched stone entryway is blocked by a heavy, studded door. I watch, detached, as my own hand reaches toward the handle, feeling no connection to it whatsoever. My gaze follows it up and I see a mirror has appeared on the door, reflecting my own face back at me.

No. It's not a mirror. It's a window.

Beyond the glass, my mirror image begins to shrink and fade, skin pulling back from bones and teeth, eyes hollowing in front of my own. The skeletal mouth wraps itself around a series of words, a rasp that fogs the glass, forming letters that I'm too scared to read. There are so many, all bleeding together, I can't tell what they say. Some of them are still there, seared into my eyelids when I wake up screaming, a horrible echo of what was spelled out on the Ouija board last week.

N-I-A-M-H, R-U-N.

28

I wake to pale sunshine and my alarm going off, my head fuzzy from more bad dreams. What did I eat last night? Was it all that baked feta?

It takes a second to realize that the noise isn't my alarm; it's my phone ringing. I roll over, bleary-eyed, to see Jess's tongue poking out at me from the screen.

Then I see the time.

Oh, nonono. I was supposed to meet her fifteen minutes ago. I scramble to pick it up.

"Hey, I'm just on my way," I lie, grabbing a pair of jeans off the floor, inching them up with one hand. "Sorry, alarm didn't go off—"

"Niamh?"

"Ruth?" I sink back down to the bed, one leg still bare. "Is everything OK?"

"It's Jess." Ruth's voice is thick and my stomach tightens. I grip the phone so hard, it hurts.

"What about her?" My voice is hoarse. "Has something happened?"

"She's in the hospital. She's been attacked."

I land at the doors of St. Mary's less than an hour later. I don't have to ask where I'm going this time, though; I've been to the ICU before.

I sprint to the elevator bank and press the button impatiently. The wait feels like an eternity. The doors eventually ping open.

"Sorry, sweetheart." A hunched old man in a hospital uniform is standing behind the bed of an even smaller man, even more hunched over. "Not much room in here. Might be best to wait for the next one."

I don't have time for this, but I remember my manners and try my best to smile.

The doors slide shut and rather than press the button again I glance around. There is a small blue sign down the hall, showing a stepped line and a little person. A stairwell. I don't hesitate; it's got to be faster than waiting.

My flip-flops slap and echo on the concrete steps. Despite my panic, I feel the loneliness of this place. I turn the corner that marks the halfway point of the first floor and see the door at the top of the next flight of steps slowly creaking closed, a dark-haired figure and familiar swish of fabric disappearing behind it.

Like the one I thought I saw at the museum, the day Tommy kissed me.

"Ignore it, ignore it," I mutter, hiding my face in my hair. It's just my mind playing tricks on me, that horrible nightmare making me see things that aren't really there. Unfortunately, my feet seem to have a mind of their own, and before I know it, I'm pushing through the same doors, finding myself in a horribly familiar, green-tiled corridor.

I'm back in the old wing.

I proceed down the corridor in a dreamlike state. It's not as quiet as it was last time and a couple brushes past me, their hushed whispers following them like a trail of smoke.

There's no dark-haired figure in sight. I knew I'd imagined it.

My feet slow down in the same place as last time, at the entrance to the wing named after Jane. I study the heavy wooden doors. They're propped open today, beckoning me in. I hesitate before taking a step into the small atrium beyond. My footsteps sound oddly hushed.

There's another set of doors leading into a dilapidated waiting room. The walls are covered in wooden panels that hint at a past grandeur, like the box at the theater, but they're brought down by shoddy PVC chairs screwed into the floor. A scattering of patients wait, quiet except for the odd sigh and the shuffle of crossing and uncrossing legs.

I shake my head. What am I doing here? I need to go and see Jess. I turn to leave, annoyed at myself and my misfiring brain for being so weird.

That's when I see him.

I hold my hands out to the glass, as though I'm going to

214

take hold of the frame, but I walk forward and squint at it instead. It's an old, faded black-and-white print, workmen in flatcaps and waistcoats, rather than helmets and reflective vests, standing in proud, neat lines in front of the old hospital wing. I glance at the tarnished plaque on the frame.

1845.

So how is he in it?

I quickly snap a photo on my phone. The resemblance really is uncanny, even though the photo is grainy. I zoom in to take another. Maybe it's just the outfit he's wearing; it's so similar to his costume. . . .

Oh, God. The museum. It's my final shift today. I check the time on my phone and realize I'm supposed to be there in an hour. I snap one final picture before spinning on my heel and leaving to go and see my friend.

"Hello, Niamh. Thank you for coming." Ruth sounds oddly formal. She has exhausted bags that stretch from under her eyes to halfway down her cheeks. She looks like she's aged ten years overnight.

"Of course." I slide in through the curtain and perch awkwardly on an empty chair. I haven't taken my backpack off, so my body is pitched forward and I put all my effort into balancing on the chair lip without falling off. I look at the figure in the bed.

Jess. She's unconscious, hooked up to a drip and some monitors that are beeping and whirring quietly in the corner.

Her normally golden-brown skin is ashy, making her look both strangely old and young at the same time. Even the smattering of freckles across her nose and cheeks seems faded.

"What happened?"

"She went out when we got home last night." A sob catches in Ruth's throat. "For milk, you know, for my tea. She's such a good girl like that. The store is only around the corner. I didn't think anything of it." She falls silent, dabbing at her red eyes with a balled-up tissue. I pull a few more sheets from the box on the table and hand them to her. She takes them hesitantly. "But then she didn't come back. I was going out to look for her when I got a call from the hospital. Someone had found her on the street and called an ambulance."

"What did the doctors say?"

"She has a concussion and a pretty nasty wound on the back of her head, but she'll be OK, they hope. Scans didn't show any swelling on the brain. They've given her a sedative, so she'll sleep." I watch as she gently strokes her daughter's hand, concern etched into the lines on her face. "She could wake up anytime," Ruth continues. "I know she wanted to talk to you. There was a half-written text on her phone."

I flush automatically, thinking about our texts.

Ruth meets my eyes. "I read them. I'm not sorry, I wouldn't have known half of it if I hadn't. The police have her phone now, anyway." She takes a deep breath. "You put her in danger, Niamh, but I only blame myself. I told her to look out for you."

An awkward silence falls between us. I stare at Jess's Afro curls, their bleached blond ends poking out from beneath what would usually strike me as a comedy-sized bandage. I feel as though my insides have been removed, carefully turned inside out, and replaced again. I want to be sick. This is my fault.

"I'm sorry," I say.

Ruth sighs. "I suppose Detective Moran called you?"

"I don't think so." I scramble for my phone and see that in fact, yes, he has. Two missed calls and a voice message fill my screen. I click on the message and hold the phone to my ear.

It only takes seconds for all the blood in my body to pool around my ankles. "Oh my God."

It's Will.

Will is out of custody.

"They released him last night, just before . . ." Ruth glances down at her daughter. "They could only keep him for twenty-four hours without a charge, and there was no real evidence against him."

"No evidence?" I echo. "So, what, he came looking for Jess right away? And no one was watching him?"

"So it seems." Silent tears streak down Ruth's bare face. "They think maybe she knew something, that he was waiting outside the house, like he did with you the other night."

"But they have him now, right?" My eyes plead for it to be true. Ruth shakes her head the tiniest bit, but it's there. No.

Will is free.

29

I stare out the window as the city zooms past, my eyes catching on every lone male on the street, just in case it's Will. Despite the fact that she must hate me now, Ruth insisted on paying for me to get a cab to the museum. She said she didn't want another attack on her conscience.

"Anywhere here is fine, thanks." The driver pulls over and I smile at him in his rearview mirror before I get out, but he completely ignores me and carries on chatting into his hands-free phone. One of the things I do not like about London. Taxi drivers are much friendlier back home.

I run down the steps, waving breathlessly at Sue, but don't get more than two feet before I'm called back to the desk.

"You're late," she says sourly.

"I know, I'm sorry, I . . ."

The phone rings and I am spared. "Never mind, never mind." She flaps a hand at me and picks up, trilling out polished professionalism. "Good afternoon, the Victorian Street Museum."

I start to sneak off, but she covers the receiver with one curled hand and hisses at me. "Hurry up, it's just you today, and Geoffrey's pulling a double shift, so he needs a break."

"I thought Tommy was working today?"

She shrugs. "He hasn't turned up." Her voice brightens again. "Ah, yes, one second, let me just put you on hold. . . ."

I leg it before she can collar me again.

I hurry into the dressing room, shrug off the cropped cardigan I'm wearing and shove it into my locker, then yank the dress off its hanger. My last shift and no Tommy. This isn't how I thought it would end.

I shimmy the dress on over my thin vest top and jeans, leaving my sneakers on. I glance down to make sure they're not visible beneath the dress and notice how worn and dirty the hem has become. Would someone else wear this after me? Would Tommy see them in it? I quickly zip myself up and take one last deep breath. This time next week, I'll either be at home or coming back in to ask for a job. I need to make a good impression.

"Excellent timing, Niamh." Geoffrey's boom is a little quieter than normal, and he follows the comment with a hacking cough. "Excuse me, dear, full of a cold. Do stay away, won't you?" He pulls out a handkerchief and proceeds to cough into it.

"I didn't realize you were sick!" I glance around the

room—it's coming up to dawn and disembodied birds chirp gaily in nonexistent trees. Icy fingers slide down my back as I realize exactly how creepy that is. "Go for your break, honestly. I'll be fine."

He doesn't argue. "Yes, thank you. Nothing a good hot whiskey won't cure, but not while I'm on duty, of course." He walks off toward the small staff kitchen. I smile at his broad retreating back and begin to count the hours away until I can go back and see Jess. I wonder if she's woken up yet.

The museum really is dead this afternoon and I'm not surprised, the weather was all kinds of amazing when I left the hospital. I pace the shadowy cobblestones like a haunted soul and my mind works overtime.

Why did the police let Will go? Did he really attack Jess? And if he did, why? What did she know? I glance around nervously and remind myself I'm safe here. There's only one way in.

Which, I realize, means there's only one way out too.

I'm pacing Jane's parlor when something vibrates near my hip, bringing me back to the now. It takes me a second to realize I still have my phone in the pocket of my jeans.

"I didn't think there was a signal down here," I mutter, glancing around furtively. There's still no one here, so I hoist up my skirt in a most unladylike fashion, hands sweaty at the thought of someone walking in and catching me, but there's no other way in this dress. I tug the phone out and let my skirts drop again.

Jess! A notification across the screen shows that she sent

me a message two minutes ago. I swipe at it, my damp fingers catching on the glass.

Awake. Head banging but OK. They're letting me go home. Need to talk to you.

I glance around again. Only Jane and I are in the room. The eyes of her unfinished portrait are following me. I start to edge away, but I quickly lose the faint signal. "Damn it." I tiptoe back toward the portrait and one lone bar springs up. I glance up and could almost swear her mouth is curving up a little more than usual. Stop it, Niamh. Of course it's not.

I tap out a response.

Thank God you're OK! At museum now. Want me to come over after?

Three little dots appear immediately, followed by a succession of rapid-fire messages.

At museum?

Is he there?

Can you leave now?

"Niamh?" Another great, racking cough travels ahead of Geoffrey into the parlor and I quickly shove my phone up my sleeve, praying it stays put.

He appears in the doorway holding a steaming cup, his bow tie, hat, and gloves gone. "Ah, there you are." He smiles at the portrait behind me and shakes his head as I feel my phone buzzing away against my arm. "Really, a most uncanny resemblance." He takes a slurp from the cup and smooths his white whiskers with his free hand. "We're going to call it a day, I'm afraid. I am sorry to do this on your last shift with us, but I need my bed and it's not worth keeping you here for the odd visitor who might happen to stumble across us."

"Oh." I feel deflated somehow. I knew today was my last day, but it feels so final.

"Now, you must promise you'll come and see me before you go home." He begins to steer me out of the parlor and I take one last look at Jane's portrait, at this girl who has infiltrated so much of my life for the last six weeks. Was this the last time I would see her?

"Of course."

"Wonderful. Now, shoo. Go and enjoy this beautiful summer's afternoon." His breath catches and he grabs his handkerchief just in time to stifle what would have been a scream-sneeze of apocalyptic measures.

"OK, thanks. Oh, and Geoffrey?" I pause at the door of the staff room. "Thanks for everything. You've been so kind, and that book you recommended for my essay was great. . . ."

"Ah, yes! Have you heard anything about that yet?"

"No, I've sent it in, but it doesn't close until Monday. I should know by the end of the week, though."

"Well, let me know how it goes, my dear. I may be able to find a more regular opening for you if you are set to become a permanent fixture here."

My heart swells a little. I really like it here. And it would mean I could keep working with Tommy. "Really?"

"Well, let's see how you get on first," he says, his eyes twinkling. He begins to walk away. "I'm locking up in ten minutes, now. See you outside."

"OK." I walk into the dressing room and untie the dress, letting it pool around my feet. I fold the crepe material carefully, smoothing out the lacy throat. It's a bit worn and sadlooking now, and, to be honest, it needs a good wash. The lace has grimy smears of makeup on it. I should get it drycleaned; that way I can give it back to Geoffrey all nice and fresh when I come back to see him.

I pack it in my bag, which I swing onto my shoulder. I look at my phone as I jog up the short flight of stairs, not wanting to keep Geoffrey from his home any longer. I can hear him talking to someone in the foyer, clearly turning some curious tourist away. My phone buzzes again. I unlock the screen to see Jess is still texting. She has completely lost her chill.

Is he there?

Niamh? Answer me, please . . .

Seriously, what are you doing? Text me back!

I start to type a response, but the three little dots are already lighting up my screen, so I wait.

Niamh, is Will there?

I freeze at the top of the stairs. Slowly, I edge closer to where Geoffrey is talking to a tall, gangly youth, his greasy hair crammed under a dark baseball cap.

Will.

I catch my breath and slide back down into the shadows, the cold of the wall biting into my back. I look around wildly for another exit, though I know there isn't one. I feel the vibration a split-second before my phone tinkles out, loud and proud, the reception back to normal now.

"Niamh?" calls Geoffrey.

I must have slipped it back on to ringer mode when I pulled it out of my sleeve.

"Er, yeah," I call, trying to keep the note of panic from my voice. "Coming."

Surely, he wouldn't do anything to Geoffrey? He was half the size of the portly older man. Did that matter if he was a psycho, though? I'll call Detective Moran. But as I swipe my phone, I see Jess's next text.

It wasn't him, Niamh! You need to trust Will. I've ordered you both another Uber—get in and don't talk to ANYONE but Will, OK?

What the hell is going on?

30

I take a deep breath and head back up the stairs, squaring my shoulders as Will comes into my line of sight. He glances at me and nods awkwardly.

"Hi." His voice is higher-pitched than I remember, and he looks drawn, ill. Geoffrey begins to say something that rapidly turns to a cough, and I shoot him a sympathetic glance.

"Hi," I mutter back, before turning to Geoffrey. "You get yourself home, now. My daddy swears by a hot whiskey with honey and cloves for a cold, and my granddaddy swore on boiled Guinness, but that sounds disgusting, don't you think?" I'm babbling, but he doesn't seem to notice.

"Yes, I think I'll skip that particular home remedy." He smiles. "This young man says he's here for you?"

I slide a sharp glance at Will. He doesn't look dangerous, just worn out. "Er, yeah, he's a . . . friend." I don't want Geoffrey telling Tommy that random guys have started dropping by for me. I spot a sleek black car slowing down outside. "In fact, I think our Uber's here. Get well soon, Geoffrey."

"Thank you, my dear."

I push the door open, humidity gathering on my skin immediately. Geoffrey locks the doors and Will gets into the car. Geoffrey begins to walk away, and I startle myself by calling out to him.

"I'll call next week," I say. "I'm going to see my friend Jess now. With Will. This guy here." I point to the car as Geoffrey furrows his brow, confused.

"Good, good," he says. "Well, bye, now."

"And then I'm off back to my dorm," I rush on, relentless, raising my voice so Will can hear me. "Last few days at college this week—I won't be missing that if I don't have to. I mean, it would look really weird if I didn't show up, wouldn't it?"

"Yes, I suppose it would." He looks totally bemused as he waves me off. But I feel calmer.

Better safe than sorry.

Will doesn't utter a word on the drive back. Jess is conveniently ignoring my texts, and by the time the cab pulls up outside our college building, I'm ready to explode.

"Why on earth would Jess come straight to the library?" I ask. "She should be in bed." Will shrugs in response and I let out a howl of frustration as I climb out and slam the door. "Fine," I mutter, stalking toward the entrance, "I'll ask her myself."

I'm aware of him trailing behind me but oddly, I don't feel threatened anymore. He's been hunched in on himself the whole way over, like someone has deflated him.

"Jess?" I swing through the door, peering through its round porthole to see the room appears empty. "Jess!" I try again.

"Back here," Jess calls from the little room where the microfilm is and I follow the sound, feeling the draft of the door as Will walks in behind me.

"Come on," I mutter, marveling as he follows me like a puppy dog. Today is weird.

"Jess!" I fly over to her chair and grab her in a bear hug without thinking.

"Ow, easy!" She laughs and I loosen up the hug. The comedy bandage is gone, but her hair is scraped back in a knotty mess and her glasses seem to magnify her bruised, tired eyes. "How are you feeling?"

"Sore," she says with a wince. "The doctor said I have some cracked ribs, but I'll be fine, I just need to rest. Look, I've made tea."

Jess fiddles with the little microfilm wheels as Will grabs himself a cup and starts to fill it.

"Tea?" I hiss. "With him? Are you going to tell me what's going on?" Jess pauses and glares at Will.

"You haven't told her?"

He takes off his hat and rubs a pale hand over his face. His eyes are bloodshot, and his chin is showing the slightest shadow of stubble. He puts a cookie in his mouth.

"Well?" Jess glares at him.

"I didn't think she'll believe me," he says, through a mouthful of crumbs. "Last time she saw me I was in her hallway, underneath a cop. Why should she listen to me?"

I lean back in my chair and fold my arms. "He's got a fair point. So?"

"Oh, hon, I . . ." To my surprise, tears slide out and pool around the base of Jess's nose. She takes her glasses off and pulls the sleeve of her red hoodie down over her hand to wipe them away. "I need to show you something."

"Show me what?" My stomach clenches and I can taste the bitter coffee I hastily downed on the way to the hospital this morning. I haven't eaten anything since last night, and combined with the scant amount of sleep I managed between speed-writing and nightmares, I'm feeling light-headed.

"It wasn't Will who attacked me last night." Jess sniffs, dabbing her eyes again before replacing her glasses. She takes a deep breath and reaches over to take my hand, wincing as she leans on a damaged rib. "Niamh, it hasn't been Will this whole time."

"So who was it, then? Jasmine? That little witch," I say.

"No, she has nothing to do with it," Will blurts, reddening slightly. "Jess told me you saw our names in the Special

Collections log. I was just . . . helping her. With the scholar-ship essay." I raise an eyebrow. "She's very persuasive."

"Then who?" I ask in a small voice.

"I need to show you," Jess repeats. "That's why I brought you here. There's something you need to see."

31

"I don't understand."

I don't. It feels impossible, ludicrous. My vision starts to blur and I watch through pinholes as Jess rips open a packet and places a cookie in my hand. "Here, eat this."

The sugar hits my system almost right away, and the edges of the room start to come back into focus. I eat it in silence, ignoring the part of my brain that's asking me how I can think of eating at a time like this, and accept the second one that Jess thrusts into my hands. She watches me like a hawk until I finish that one too and I lick the melted chocolate from my thumb. She nods.

"Good girl. Will, put some sugar in her tea. No arguments, Niamh."

"OK." I accept the mug from him gratefully. Heat floods into my hands, chasing away the pins and needles, and I start to feel human once more.

"Are you sure?" I say.

"Yeah." She pulls her hoodie tighter around her. I notice the end of a hospital bracelet poking out from under one of the cuffs.

He put my friend in the hospital. I trusted him.

"But why?"

"I'm not certain." She turns back to the microfilm again. "But I have an idea. There has been some pretty weird stuff happening, hasn't there?"

"Supernatural happenings," Will intones heavily.

"Will, this is the problem," Jess snaps. "You skulk around here, keep showing up in the worst places, and then you come out with comments like that."

"The theater," I interrupt, thinking of the Man in Gray's burning eyes in the stalls.

"Er, that was me," Will says guiltily.

"Excuse me?"

"Yeah." Will rubs the back of his neck with one gangly arm. "I was only trying to help. The same as when you saw me outside your place, I was trying to protect you." He at least has the grace to look sheepish as I clasp my mug tighter, hearing it creak under the strain.

"You scared the living daylights out of me!"

He doesn't reply, just looks at the floor.

"Anyway," Jess breaks the silence. "He's right. Weird—supernatural—stuff, has been happening." She swivels around in her chair to face us. "You know, I always thought I wanted ghosts and stuff to be real. Now? Not so sure." She sighs and pauses, swinging back to resume scrolling. "Here. I still don't know if I do believe my own eyes, but—well, you tell me what you think."

She clicks a few times, and a grainy black-and-white image sharpens. It's a Victorian street scene. "Look."

I lean in and squint. As if by magic, the scene clarifies itself, and I realize she's playing with the filters.

"Tell me what you see."

I don't have to. I've spotted him right away, or someone who looks an awful lot like him. He's standing in the corner of the frame, dressed as a paper boy, holding a newspaper in the air.

"Wait." I reach into my bag for my phone and pull up the photo I snapped earlier. The one I had forgotten about until now. I find it and use my fingers to zoom in as far as I can, before propping the phone up next to the screen.

"Where did you get this?"

I quickly explain about the hospital this morning. I'm tempted to leave out the bit about following a figure, but screw it. I'm going all in.

"And I think . . . I think Jane Alsop has got something to do with this."

Jess looks at me sharply. "Jane? Dead girl from 1838, Jane?"

"Yeah. I . . . had a bad dream." I wince as I say the words out loud. "She was trying to warn me."

"A dream?" Will says. He leans forward in his chair, looking animated for the first time ever.

I start to explain the dream about the graveyard, the

feeling I got when I went near the occult artifacts at the museum, the glimpse of a dress in the hospital this morning that led me to the photograph. "And my phone," I realize. "Earlier today, at the museum. I always leave my phone in my locker, because there's no signal down there, but today I didn't."

"What's so weird about that?"

"It started working when I was in the parlor. When I was right in front of Jane's portrait."

"She's trying to help you," Will murmurs.

Jess shakes her head. "Could just be a co— Will, where are you going?" His chair legs squeak on the floor as he quickly pushes it back and disappears through the door into the main library. Jess looks at me in exasperation. "Seriously, no wonder we suspected him."

"Here." A large, thin book crashes down on the desk, announcing Will's return. Jess rolls her eyes at me.

"See?" she mutters.

I look down and see it's the scrapbook I saw that day in the library, the one he snatched away from me. Will leans over me to open it and I slide my chair back. I'm still not completely comfortable with him this close to me.

"What is this?" The first page is covered in clippings from ancient newspapers. ("Photocopies—not originals, I hope," Jess grumbles under her breath.) I study them and reach out to turn the page, revealing a familiar double spread. My finger pauses on the ink drawing, a man dressed up like a devil, arms outstretched, batlike wings protruding from them.

"I've seen this before." I rack my brain, trying to shake the memory loose. Something about Punch and Judy, or the theater . . . Wait. I've got it. "Spring-Heeled Jack?"

Will looks positively delighted. Jess, on the other hand, does not.

"Come on, Will, explain." She points at Jack's sneering, mustachioed face, and then at the two pictures of the boy who looks so heart-wrenchingly familiar. "What's this guy got to do with this guy?"

"I think they're all the same person." He's so serious, I can't help it. I start to laugh again, but the solemn look on his face makes the sound die in my throat. "Really. Look." He flips through the book once more, and I see he's not only collected articles about Jack, but his victims. Attacks from as far back as October 1837 litter the pages, some accompanied by sketches, and, as the cuttings become more modern, photographs, first in black-and-white and then color. The last ones are dated from this month, and the smiling, earnest faces of Sara and Tasha beam up at me. I can see that someone, presumably Will, has drawn a small black cross and a neat inscription next to the photo of Sara. Deceased.

"OK," I say slowly, desperately trying to fit the jigsaw pieces together. "So there have been all these attacks over, what, the last two centuries, pretty much?" Will nods and leans back in his chair as Jess studies the book. "That's interesting and all, but how do they all link together? How do you have him down as Spring-Heeled Jack?" I flip back to the first page and point to a heading: *The Terror of London?* "He's only . . ." I hesitate. "Well, he's not that *old,*" I finish weakly.

I have no idea how old he is.

"Look at the date, Niamh." Will points to the first article, and I skim it.

"Yeah, February 1838. So?"

"There was another attack, Lucy Scales. Happened one week after Jane died, near a traveling fairground."

"Ah," Jess chimes in, her eyes sparking. "If he was some ghoulie murdering revenant, wouldn't he have started with Jane?"

Will's eyes narrow. "I thought we were on the same side."

"We are, we are." Jess holds up her hands, the hospital band on full display now. "I'm just playing devil's advocado, that's all. I am, first and foremost, a woman of science, you know."

"Right." Will flips the page back to the pictures of the girls I'm so familiar with, the ones who could have— should have—been my friends. "If *I'm* going to play devil's advocate—"

"Whatever," she grumbles.

"—then I'd go with the revenant angle."

"Really?" Jess perks up.

"Yeah, I know it's crazy, but hey." He gestures to the scrapbook. I must look bewildered. "A revenant," he explains gently, "is kind of like a vicious vampire . . ."

Jess nearly snorts out her tea. "No, it's not!"

"OK, what is it, then?"

"It's more like a ghost—a romantic, yearning . . ."

"It really isn't."

"It is! Haven't you read those Amy Plum books? The ones set in Paris?" Jess fake-swoons and Will starts to argue with her.

I sigh and Google "revenant."

" 'A revenant,' " I read aloud in a flat monotone, " 'is an animated corpse that is believed to have been revived from death to haunt the living. It comes from the Old French *revenant,* the *returning* or *revenir, to come back.'* " I put my phone down and thank the gods of Wikipedia. "Sound about right?"

"Whatever," says Will. "Anyway, revenants have this connection with people, this ability to bring them back."

"Er, OK. So why is he doing the opposite? Why is he hurting people?" I hurry to correct myself. "I mean, if you're right, which would be very, very weird, why has he been attacking girls?"

"Girls who look like you," Will corrects.

"No," I protest. "Not all of them. Me and Jess look nothing alike."

"Yeah, but I was attacked for a different reason," says Jess. "He was different. Cold. Almost . . . dead behind the eyes. He must have known that I recognized him, that I'd match him up with the microfilm pictures eventually."

"Which you did," I say.

Jess nods. "He thought I was going to tell you about all this, and he wanted me out of the way."

I don't say anything. I can't believe what I'm hearing. Not only are they telling me that one of the people I trusted most while I was here has been behind all this, but that he is some kind of ancient, bloodthirsty undead person too.

The real problem is . . . I think I'm starting to believe them.

"There are more pictures, Niamh," Jess says quietly. She flips to another one. There he is again, head slightly down, but unmistakable.

"Are you sure they're not all long-lost relatives?" I try.

"They could be, I guess," Jess says, flipping to yet another picture, the background of which I recognize. The museum. It's in color, this one, but the outfits are all in shades of yellow and brown, so I mark it down as some time in the 1970s. It's the front of the museum, and an old man is proudly cutting a ribbon with some huge, metal-handled scissors. "This one did make me wonder, whether it was a relative or not, but here's one more."

She flips to a magazine article, this one definitely from the 1990s. It shows a nightclub, a lush, velvet sofa, and a slim brunette sitting on his lap. I recognize the woman and flip back to a page in the Will's eerie scrapbook. Yes, there she is. A perfectly symmetrical, angular face stares out at me, lips lined in '90s brown, her hair long and shiny, parted in the middle. *"Remembering the tragic teenage supermodel, Caitlin Cooke, on the twenty-fifth anniversary of her murder."*

"No," I whisper, pushing the book away. "No."

"Niamh, don't you see? I think he's in these photos on

purpose. Can you imagine how hard it was to get into a photograph back in Victorian times? When Jane died, they were only just being invented! He could have done it to keep some kind of warped record of his existence. He must have a weird obsession with them—I mean, all those pictures of you asleep. He must have taken them. Then deleted them when you were downstairs."

So he was there all the time. I shiver.

"But . . ."

My phone begins to flash, making me jump. It's just Meghan trying to FaceTime.

"Ignore it," I say, shaking my head. I'll call her later.

"OK," Jess plows on, "and Will told me this morning that he noticed something else."

"A pattern," Will supplies. "Between the pictures we found of him and the dates of the attacks."

"And?"

"They match. But more than that, there's a definite pattern. He attacks five girls in total, generally leaving at least the last one dead. Then he's off the radar."

"For how long?" My phone starts to buzz again. "Sorry, it's my sister. My granny hasn't been well."

"Answer it," Jess says kindly. She drains the dregs of the teapot into our cups as I swipe the screen and walk over to the corner.

"Hey, Megs," I say quietly as her flushed, beaming face fills the screen. "Is everything OK? It's not a great time, can I call you back?" She starts to giggle, and I notice a view

I've grown very familiar with over the last few weeks in the background. "Megs." I hear the warning tone in my voice. "Where are you?"

"SURPRISE!" she shouts, spinning around, the South Bank whizzing past behind her. "I'm in London!"

"What?" Oh, Jesus, how has she managed this one? "Do Mom and Daddy know?"

"Not yet, but I left a note when they went to get Granny out of the hospital. You know what it's like, having to drive to Dublin and back, it takes the whole day. I was at the airport and on the plane before they even landed at St. Vincent's." Her smile drops slightly. "They'll skin me alive when I get back but it's gonna be soooo worth it. Hey!" She swivels the phone to show a tall figure dressed in black, walking a few paces ahead of her, and then pans back. "I went to your museum to surprise you, but it was shut. I wasn't sure what to do. Your friend was there, though!" She lowers her voice conspiratorially, bringing the phone to her mouth so all I can see is a close-up of her lips. "I know he's older, but he's a hottie, Niamh, why didn't you say?"

Blood freezes in my veins.

"Meghan, listen to me . . ."

"I'll see you in a minute, anyway. How lucky am I, coming to a party on my first night?"

"Party? What party? Megs, *listen,* you shouldn't be going off with strangers. . . ."

"Sorry, *Mommy,*" she laughs, pulling the phone away. "He's not a stranger, though, is he? You know him. Look, I

239

think we're nearly here, he said it wasn't far from this place." My stomach contracts as I see the gates of the same graveyard we walked past the other night looming up behind her.

I'm going to be sick.

"Meghan, get away from him now. Turn around and run the other way. Go into a shop or a bar or something, anywhere with people." Her face slowly falls as she realizes I'm serious.

"But he said he was taking me to meet you." Her voice is small, and I remember how big a gap those eleven months between us can feel sometimes. "He said we were going to a party at your friend's house." The screen is jumping and I can tell she's walking away, fast. Good girl.

"Whose house did he say he was taking you to?"

"Oh." Her breath is coming out faster now. "Jane's, I think?"

I'm vaguely aware that Will and Jess are flanking me, watching the scene unfold over my shoulder. Jess's hand flies to her mouth.

"It's fine," I soothe, trying to keep her calm. "We just, ah, we had a falling-out, that's all. I don't want you around him right now."

"OK." She pauses and looks down at the screen, her voice thick, panicked. "I can't see anywhere to go, Niamh. I think I've gone the wrong way!"

"Just keep going, we'll find you, don't worry." Jess is already ordering an Uber and I motion for Will to grab our stuff. "I'm on my way to get you now, just stay there." I follow my friends out of the library, my voice low as we sneak past Ruth's office, keeping my eyes on Meghan the whole way. "Can you see him?"

"No." The picture wobbles as she hurries along. "How long will you be?"

"Fifteen minutes; we just need to cross the river. Megs, can you hear me?"

Her phone thuds to the ground just as our car pulls up outside.

"Meghan? Meghan! Pick up the phone!"

The screen begins to lurch, and a face finally comes into view. Only, it's not the familiar face of my sister.

Tommy cuts the phone off right as I start to scream.

32

I know the tapping of my nails on the console between me and the driver must be driving him nuts, but I can't help it. The journey feels ten times longer than usual and no one is picking up the phone, Derek and Detective Moran nowhere to be found. Plus, to make matters worse, Meghan's phone isn't even ringing, which means it's off.

Or broken.

"Here!" I don't wait for the car to stop fully before I hurl myself out onto the pavement, ignoring the angry shout of the driver. I stumble slightly, a horn blaring at me as I run blindly across the road. I right myself and race toward the cemetery entrance, my eyes on the low wall where I last saw Meghan. She's not there.

"Niamh, wait!" Jess and Will appear next to me as the car squeals away.

"She's gone." My voice is dull, which is weird, because

something molten is rising from my stomach. "SHE'S GONE!" I scream, aiming a foot at the gray stones.

"Whoa, stop!" Jess catches me and holds on tight as I immediately sag into her arms. "This won't do any good, will it? You need to be strong, for Meghan. OK?"

"OK," I snivel into my arm. "You're right. But what now?" I sink down to the pavement, mimicking what I'd seen my sister do only minutes ago. It seems like hours. I trace my finger across a sparkling patch of pavement and lift it up to the light, wondering if the tiny shards of glass clinging to my skin have come from her phone.

"Tell us again, what exactly did she say?"

"He said he was taking her to meet me. At Jane's party."

"At Jane's party?" Will repeats.

"Yes. Well, a party at Jane's house."

Will frowns. "But Jane Alsop lived at the museum."

"Wait." Jess is staring over the cemetery wall, past the lumbering iron gates. "Tell us about the dream you had again."

"The graveyard one?" I rub my face. "Um, that I was walking through it to a kind of little building."

"Like that one?"

I stand up so fast, my head spins, and I have to lean on the rough brick wall to stop myself from falling over. "Which one?" I follow Jess's pointing finger and see a short, stumpy building. It's shaped like a kid's drawing of a house, a pointed roof but no chimney or windows. A weathered metal door is set into the middle and it looks run-down, neglected.

"Kind of." I try to conjure the nightmarish image in my head. "But it was, I dunno, fancier than that one. Prettier, you know? Like, it had columns and stuff on it."

"And a window?" Will is busy scrolling on his phone.

"Yeah." The image of the sunken face, ropes of rotten hair framing it, scorches into my mind. "Yeah, there was a window."

"Would you recognize it?" he asks, still tapping.

"What? But it wasn't real. . . ." I fall silent as he holds up his phone and I see the building from my dream there, on the screen in all its Technicolor glory.

"Of course," whispers Jess. "Where Jane was buried."

"I told you." Will locks the phone and smiles at me grimly. "She's been trying to help you. What you saw, in your dream, that was Jane's mausoleum."

"Oh my God."

"Plus," he adds, nodding over the wall, "guess where it is?"

"No," I breathe. Was that where Tommy was trying to take me the other night?

"Yes." He lifts his chin and for the first time, I see something like confidence in his eyes. "It's somewhere in there. And I think that's where he's taken your sister."

"How big is this place?" I mutter.

"Few acres, I think." Will's voice is muffled by the

stagnant atmosphere. I follow him deeper into the graveyard, brambles and old, dried flowers that have been shifted by the wind crunching beneath my feet. The air is soupy here, full of static electricity. Low, gray clouds have gathered, effectively blocking out the last of the afternoon sun. It feels like a storm cloud is following us.

Jess is lagging behind. I stop to let her catch up as Will plows ahead. She's clutching her ribs and there's a sheen of sweat on her forehead. The trees winding above us seem to knit closer together as the gloom settles around our shoulders.

"You OK?" I ask.

She nods, but her eyes are welling up. "I just . . ."

"What?"

Her voice comes out in a strained whisper. "I just don't think I can face him so soon. I'm sorry, Niamh."

"Hey, hey." I try to shush her sniffles and she bites back a sob. "I get it. It's scary. But, Jess . . . she's my baby sister."

"I know," she says, taking a deep breath. "I know."

"Hey, you two," a voice hisses from the crooked grave-stones ahead of us. "What are you doing?" Will appears from behind a tall, moss-covered angel. It doesn't have a head.

"Have you found it?" I hiss back, wrapping my fingers around Jess's, her palm sweaty in mine.

"No, but we must be getting close." He brushes a crooked headstone with one finger, moving clumps of moss away. "Eighteen fifty." He points back the way we came. "The ones over there were a bit newer, and the ones farther in tend to be older. They started from the inside out." He glances at Jess. "Is she OK?"

"No. She doesn't want to see him."

"I don't blame her." He surprises me by speaking to Jess clearly and calmly, like she's a little kid. "Hey, Jess? Why don't you wait at the entrance?"

"What?" Her eyes refocus on him. "No, you need my help, I . . ."

"You will be helping," he continues. "You need to go and call your mom and Detective Moran, tell them what's happened. Can you do that for me?"

"Great idea," I agree, spinning her gently and giving her a push toward the entrance, itching to get to my sister.

"Y-yes, OK," she mutters, glancing back over her shoulder. "Are you sure?" Her mouth is set, but her eyes are pleading with me to let her go.

"Yeah, it's a good idea. Just don't tell them any of the, you know, weird stuff."

She nods. "Good idea."

I study Will's face before giving Jess's retreating figure one last glance. Maybe after all this, he is working with Tommy. Luring me deeper into the graveyard. He wouldn't send Jess for the police if he was in on it, would he? Maybe he's pulling a double bluff, though, to get me on my own, and . . .

"Niamh?" He snaps his fingers in front of my face. "Are you ready?"

"Yes."

I have no other choice.

"This is it."

The sky has settled even lower now, so when we reach the mausoleum, it's covered in heavy, creeping shadows. The gray stone building rears up from tangles of brambles and dead, spindly bushes. Branches reach into the gray sky like knotted white bones and I shudder, thinking of the dead face I saw through this window. I remember the letters scored into my mind's eye after I woke up.

N-I-A-M-H. R-U-N.

Will heads around to the other side, his sneakers crunching through the loose gravel. I wince, trying my best to walk weightlessly toward the columns that arch up toward the domed roof of the crypt. It's the largest monument in this part of the graveyard. I can see how the weeping statue above the door was once beautiful, but eighteen decades of relentless London rain have sloughed off the finely carved features. Now there's nothing but a blank, empty face staring down at me.

I approach the door. It's made from heavy, greenish metal and a huge fleur-de-lis sits in the center. A handle, I think. Small patches of orange flowers litter the ground around the doorway, and my heart sinks as I think of the day Tommy taught me about flowers and their meanings. I think this is butterfly weed. I've seen it at home on Granny's old farm.

I wonder what it means.

I turn my attention back to the door, where mottled green studs march up either side; it looks like it's never supposed to be opened.

So of course, I push it.

Nothing.

"Anything?"

I clap my hand over a scream as Will's voice fills my ear.

"Jesus!" I hiss. My heart is thumping out of control. "No. It won't open."

"Let me try."

I stand aside and watch as Will leans a scrawny shoulder into the door. I roll my eyes and leave him to it, picking my way around the opposite side. That's when I see it.

A window.

It's not in the same place and it's higher than I remember, though I guess even creepy prophetic ghost dreams can be inaccurate that way. Everything else is the same, though. A square, deep-set window. Bars on the outside. Scratched, dirty glass beyond them.

I need to see through that window.

"Will," I hiss. He pops his head around the corner, sweat beading on his upper lip. "Look." I point to the window and he nods, lacing his hands together without a second thought.

"Need a boost?"

I brace myself on the wall, stepping into his knotted fingers. "Ready?" He nods and I push myself up, grabbing hold of a bar with my free hand. I can feel him struggling already. I let my eyes adjust to the gloom inside the mausoleum and scan around for any sign of Meghan.

"I can't see her." I hold on to the bars with both hands now. I crane my neck around to peer at a corner and see a foot. And that foot is attached to a body.

But not my sister's body.

From my vantage point, I can just about make out the male figure sitting in the corner, clutching a pile of rags in his arms, the way a mother would hold a newborn baby. I squint as Will wobbles precariously under me. I'm running out of time. Where is Meghan?

A shaft of late-afternoon sun bursts through the low clouds, illuminating Tommy like some kind of fallen angel. That is when I catch a glimpse of the curved, skeletal hands protruding from Tommy's bundle.

He's embracing nothing but bones.

33

My hand slips on the bar. Will can't hold me anymore and we fall. The crash of our two bodies hitting the ground rumbles through the graveyard like thunder. I spring to my feet, praying to Saint Anthony that Jess has reached the police, before remembering he's the patron saint of lost things and not victims of crazed maniacs.

The heavens open then, sending huge torrents of rain down, fast and furious, plastering my hair and clothes to my skin immediately. I stride around to the doorway.

"Help me!" I scream at Will, trying to make myself heard over the rain and readying myself to slam into the door. But I don't need his help.

Instead, the door creaks open from the inside.

"You shouldn't have come here." Tommy fills the doorway, and it's his voice, but not like I've ever heard it before. It's dull and thick and . . . cruel. I've never heard him sound like that.

"Meghan?" My voice is stronger than I thought it would be, and I'm glad. I can't let him know how scared I am.

"She's here." He backs out of the entrance and a shaft of gray light fills the little structure, the rain stopping as suddenly as it started. Meghan's limp body is stretched out next to some kind of plinth, facedown on the floor. I run toward her without thinking and pull her head into my lap.

"Meghan!" I brush graveyard dirt from her smooth cheeks and shake her gently. She's pale, too pale, and the crook of my arm beneath her head is starting to grow sticky and warm.

"You monster," I grind out, baring my teeth at him. "What have you done to her?"

"She was making too much noise." He says it almost casually, like giving someone a head injury to keep them quiet is the most natural thing in the world. "I had to shut her up."

I shake Meghan's body gently, then a little harder when I don't get a response. She protests against me, her eyes rolling behind their lids. She's alive.

I take my eyes off my sister and have a proper look at Tommy for the first time. He's more disheveled than I've seen him, filthy and haggard-looking. It's hard to believe that this is the same fresh-faced boy I thought I was falling in love with. Was this really my first love? Talk about tragic.

He skulks back to the dark corner and sits down, in a world of his own, stroking the tattered cloth that holds who knows what inside of it. I chance a glimpse at the door and spot Will in the shadow of the doorway. Tommy hasn't noticed him yet. I hold up my hand to stall him and he nods, then ducks back, phone in hand.

I need him to get Meghan out of here.

Tommy is bent over his bundle. My eyes try their best to make out shapes and objects, but nothing is familiar to me. Well, one thing is, but I'm trying not to look at the open, empty coffin on the plinth above my head.

"Meghan?" I press my lips to my sister's ear, trying to rouse her. "Megs? Can you hear me? I need you to wake up."

"I can't let you do that." All at once, Tommy is standing over me, clutching the sides of the coffin now, his bare knuckles white against the aging wood. He didn't make a sound. He's looking down on me with sad eyes, but there's something detached about them too. Like this is nothing personal. "I told you," he says with a sigh. "You shouldn't have come. You were finally safe."

"Safe?" My fury bubbles to the surface. I trusted him. I *kissed* him! "You killed Sara, attacked Tasha, Jess. That girl in the Underground?"

"I never harmed you, did I?"

"You've made my life a waking nightmare!" I seethe, reliving each and every moment of panic from the last six weeks in one fell swoop. "How dare you." Tears are falling from my eyes now, splashing onto Meghan, smearing the dust on her face into thin gray rivulets. "How dare you do all this, and then tell me I'm safe."

"I'm sorry." His voice is dull again, void of life, of expression. "But I had to do it. You don't understand." He begins to

252

arrange the tattered brown flowers that make up an ancient funeral wreath at the head of the coffin, attempting to plump them up. I squint to get a better look at the sections of long brown material decorating the coffin and bile rises in the back of my throat when I realize what it is.

It's hair. Human hair.

I lay Meghan down gently and stand on wobbly legs as the memorials scattered around the crypt sharpen into focus. Wreaths, long fernlike wings, and small pieces of hair braided into jewelry decorate the floor around the central coffin. The coffin itself is lined with moth-eaten velvet, clearly once red but now faded to the color of a soft rosebud lip. Small stoppered bottles litter the interior of the casket, their thick, green glass nestled in the folds of threadbare material. "What is all this?"

"Magic." He almost smiles, as if all this is funny. "Sorcery. Witchcraft. Mesmerism. Demonology. Call it what you like. But I told you, you won't understand."

"Then explain it to her." Will's voice comes from the doorway. I look at him, urging him to stay back, but he shakes his head at me, almost imperceptibly. "She might understand, if you explain." He begins to inch inside, and I see that he's getting closer to Meghan.

Maybe this could work after all.

"Well?" I try to look interested as my skin crawls and the moisture drains from my lips. Who knew this would be when my acting skills came in handy? I turn back to Tommy. "Explain," I say. "Why have you been doing this? Why have you been stalking me?" My voice drops. "I could have loved you, you know."

"I KNOW!" he roars, letting go of the wreath and smashing it to the floor in an explosion of anger, splinters of wood from the stand hurtling across the crypt. Will jumps in front of Meghan to protect her from the crash and pulls her limp body out of the way. Tommy throws another wreath, and another and another, finally reaching for one of the small bottles. He snatches his hand back, as though the glass is hot, and drops to the floor, his pale hands twisted in his hair. "I know," he repeats, rocking back and forth. "But I had to do it, it's the only way." He crawls over to the bundle of bones discarded in the corner and lifts them up, ever so gently. They crunch and rasp together as he embraces them, and I feel sick all over again.

"The only way to what?"

"To bring her back," Will says. He takes a step toward the coffin, stepping around the strands of long-dead hair that now decorate it, like some kind of macabre party streamers. "You've been trying to bring her back all this time, haven't you? You stole the grimoire and the tarot cards from the museum."

"They were mine," Tommy mutters weakly.

Will continues, ignoring him. "You were her secret love, weren't you? The one she snuck down to meet the night she died."

"Yes," Tommy chokes out.

"Are you serious?" I look at Jane's empty coffin and back

down at the boy clutching her skeleton as though his own life depends on it. "But how? I mean, you should be . . ."

"Dead?" He gives a flat laugh. "You're right. Many, many times over. But love can do strange things to you. Throw in a bit of magic and a mother with the lineage of a witch and it's amazing what you can achieve."

I hear Meghan stirring behind me.

"Niamh?" Her weak voice manages. I try to mask her sounds, filling the mausoleum with my voice.

"So you were lovers?" I inch around the coffin and slowly move to where he's sitting. It's a gruesome scene, the object of my affection crying over a dead body, but if it keeps him busy, Will can get Meghan out of here.

"We were going to get married," he tells me, stroking a finger across one hollow cheekbone, like he once did to me. Twice, I realize, remembering the caress when I was trapped in the library. A shudder travels down my spine as I crouch in front of him and try to keep him talking. "That's why she was meeting me that night. We were going to run away together. Elope." The ghost of a smile tickles his lips. "We were so happy. And then . . ."

"Then she had the accident."

He nods, a sob escaping from his lips as his clutch on the body tightens. "She'd hidden some coins, some jewelry, things we could sell, behind one of the machines. She went to get them and somehow she turned on the mechanism, and . . . and . . ." He picks up a clump of hair from the floor and tries to place it on her skull, but it just slides back down into the dust. "She got dragged in." He stares down at the body, as though he's shocked it's there. "And she died."

"It wasn't your fault." I try to sound sympathetic, but it's hard when your fight-or-flight is screaming at you to get out. I take the chance to glance back at Will and see that he has a very wobbly Meghan up on her feet. My heart soars as he guides her through the doorway, and I quickly turn back and keep talking. "There was nothing you could do."

"I tried, don't you see?" He gestures around to the odd collections stuffed into little nooks around the mausoleum, bottles and wreaths and jars shoved haphazardly into crevices. "The book told me I could bring her back."

"Who gave you the book?"

Tommy gently readjusts his bundle of bones, and, still cradling it, moves toward a central wreath. My eyes are adjusting now, and I see the hair is looped and swirled around a small brown book. Little shapes that look like stars are carved into the cover.

"My mother."

I swear I can hear the pieces clicking together in my brain. "Your mother. She was Madame Josephine?"

Tommy nods and picks up the book, reverently turning the pages. His action dislodges two ancient black cards that flutter gently to my feet. I bend my knees and feel for them on the floor, refusing to take my eyes off him. I find and pick up the missing cards from the tarot deck in the museum. Two more faintly gilded skeletons, one holding a skull and a scythe, and the other resplendent in an elaborate crown, grin up at me before they are snatched from my grip.

"I need those." Tommy places the open grimoire back on its stand and fusses with the placement of the cards. "The Empress," he mumbles, "and Death. For love and new beginnings."

"But it never worked, did it?"

"No." He looks back up at me with something like pain in his gaze. "It didn't. And my mother died—I couldn't go back and undo it. I'm . . . stuck."

"Stuck?"

"In this body. And I won't be able to move on until I bring her back, don't you see? I knew I could do it this time, I just needed certain . . . items."

"Like what?" The words almost stick in my throat as images from the last few weeks parade in front of my eyes. I think I already know what he's going to say.

"The tarot cards. Hair, for remembrance and renewal." Sara's poor, broken body flashes through my mind, the bald patches on her beautiful head standing out in stark relief as Tommy traces his finger along the parchment. "Fingernails." Tasha's bare, bloody nailbeds follow in the morbid slideshow my memories are creating. "For strength and sharpness of wit."

"Let me guess the next one . . . an eye?" I gulp. He nods as I see in my mind the girl on the Underground clutching her bloody face.

"So she could see the world again." He's reeling the list off as though it's a recipe he's more than familiar with, one he's followed time and time again. He doesn't need the book. I wonder how many lives he has ruined trying to fix his own.

"What else?" I ask, my curiosity now taking over.

"A piece of jewelry that was special to its wearer, for sentiment and an open heart," he drones, his words muffled in the lace of Jane's rotting gown. He looks up at me with wide eyes. "I got that one before I met you. I think, maybe, if I'd have met you sooner . . ."

"What? You wouldn't have done any of this?" He slumps back down to the floor and I see how pathetic and broken he really is. "So where do I come into all this, then?"

"You were the final piece. But I . . . I couldn't do it." He slams a hand on the floor and I choke on the dust that rises around us, trying not to think about what I might be breathing in. "I knew that this time, if I did it, if I . . . used you, it would finally work. Because I cared about you." Tommy tries to stretch a hand toward me and I flinch away without thinking. "I couldn't hurt you, though. I couldn't use you."

"Use me?" Is that a siren in the distance? "What do you mean, use me? Is that why you took Meghan, to use her instead?" I press. "What's the final thing you need, Tommy?"

He's too fast on his feet and I realize, too late, that he's been playing me. Before I can react, he drops Jane's lifeless bones to the floor and wraps his hand around my ponytail, dragging me up to standing by my hair. My vision starts to tunnel as pressure builds around the base of my neck, where he's holding me with one strong hand.

"A heart, my beautiful Niamh. Your warm and beating heart."

34

I come to, blinking slowly, my eyes and throat dry and dusty. I'm lying flat on my back, staring into the dark, domed roof of the mausoleum, its little rectangular indentations messing with my vision. I close my eyes again and try to push myself up, but my arms and legs are constricted. I am wrapped in something slippery and soft, covering me from neck to toes. I stretch and glance down as far as I can.

I'm in Jane's funeral shroud.

And I'm not alone.

"Tommy?" I say. I try to force down the panic but *Oh God, oh God, oh God,* I'm in a coffin and there's a dead girl crammed in here next to me.

"Shush, it's fine." A cool hand reaches out to stroke my brow and I flinch. "It's nearly over, not long now." I swivel my head around desperately, trying to shake the stinking shroud off me. I can see that Tommy is re-erecting the main wreath again, piecing bits of hair back together, wrapping the tarot cards in it. Hard lumps press into the back of my head and my hands, and I realize I'm lying on top of those little glass bottles. My stomach recoils as I realize what must be in them.

"Tommy." My voice comes out pleading, broken. "Please. You don't have to do this. We . . ."

" 'We'?" He laughs harshly, grabbing the edge of the coffin and peering down at me. "There is no 'we,' Niamh. Don't you see? You're here for a higher purpose, to sacrifice yourself, so she can finally come back!" I see tiny white flecks of foam start to gather at the corners of his mouth. "Now shut up. I'm trying to concentrate."

I close my eyes and try to recall all the stupid horror movies that Meghan has ever made me watch. Ironically, she'd probably be great in this situation, the one I've saved her from.

I start to spread my fingers out as Tommy mills around, setting up his horrific little altar. I hear a familiar clink of metal and a stream of sunlight flashes off the sharp set of curved, metal nails—*claws*—that Tommy is ceremoniously sliding onto his fingers. Tears roll down the side of my face.

"Why the nails?" I choke out.

Tommy turns to me and leans closer, tracing a finger down my face, only this time it's hard, sharp, and I feel the white-hot pain of the claw's knife-sharp edge parting my flesh and the warm rush of blood run down my cheek.

"These?" he asks innocently. "I suppose you could say they were part of the original costume."

"Costume? You're actually him, aren't you? Spring-Heeled Jack."

"What a ridiculous name," he snorts, removing his hand from my face. "People can be so stupid. Have you read some of those stories?"

"I don't understand." I need to keep him talking. As he does, I work one hand out of the shroud, slowly enough to escape his notice.

"You wouldn't," he sneers. His handsome face has long departed, and I wonder if it was ever there in the first place. "It started as a way to be separate from it all. I could do these"—he waves at the grimoire—"*things* as someone else. The newspaper industry was booming then and as soon as they got wind of the attacks, they created a monster."

I pat around frantically with my free hand and it lands on long, spindly fragments that can only be Jane's fingers. I pull away automatically, a sharp, searing pain slashing into my fingertips.

Wait.

Bones are sharp too.

"Sorry, Jane," I whisper, gasping out a raspy cough to cover the sound of snapping bone as I wrench one finger off. Tommy ignores me, so I carry on, maneuvering the now needle-sharp bone inside the shroud.

"But it was you all along?" I ask. "Spring-Heeled Jack, the Terror of London."

"I suppose so," he mumbles, engrossed in his gruesome task. "Though I couldn't scale ten-foot walls or breathe blue fire. I might be immortal, but I've still had to do things the hard way. It's all lies."

I cough again and thrust the finger bone upward. A small indentation appears in the cloth, but no hole, so I persevere, wiggling it around until a shard of yellowing calcium pokes through. Adrenaline floods through me as I feel the brittle material begin to rip. I start to cough again, desperately trying to mask the tear of threads ripping through the little cavernlike room until my entire arm is free and I can see the outline of Jane's remains curled up by my side.

"What are you . . ." Tommy leans over the casket again, his claws wrapped around the lip of the coffin, but I'm too fast for him this time. I lift my hand, wielding the spiked shard of bone, and, before I can overthink it, I plunge it deep into the side of his neck. He looks at me for a second, his mouth a little circle of surprise, before I wrench it out. Horror-movie tip number one: never drop your weapon.

Dark, viscous liquid sprays out across the wall and Tommy clasps a hand to the wound, looking at the blood in shock. I take my chance and jump, throwing my full weight at him, thrusting my shoulder into his chest as hard as I can. I tumble myself and the contents of the casket down on top of him and watch in slow motion as the little, stoppered bottles and the final mortal remains of Jane Alsop explode across the floor. Tommy gapes at me in horror, blood spurting from between his fingers.

"NO!"

I try to push myself off him, but I've landed awkwardly, my arm at a crazy angle. I stagger to my feet. My arm dangles down at my side, floppy and useless.

"No! Look what you've done!" His tears are genuine now, floods of salty regret mixing with the blood still trickling from his neck. He's sweeping the fragments of bone together, desperately trying to put her together again, smearing his blood across the floor, mixing it in with the dirt.

"It's over, Tommy," I whisper. He looks up at me with huge, wet eyes. His skin is dulling quickly, his hair turning from sandy to gray right in front of me. "You need to leave her to rest. She's not coming back." I choke back a sob. "*You* need to rest."

"Over?" he repeats, his lips thinning by the second. I nod and he fumbles in his pocket, pulling out something that he rolls across the floor to me. "It's really over?"

"I think so. I think you just need to accept that she's not coming back." I pick the object out of the dust with my good hand and rub my thumb across it, lifting the lid with a click. It's a small glass cylinder with a large lever on the top and I realize it's an old type of lighter, like the one Geoffrey said had been stolen. I realize what the girl in my nightmare— Jane, I remind myself, watching Tommy weep into her broken body—was trying to tell me. She wasn't warning me to run, I just didn't see at the time. I do now. The letters seem to merge before my eyes and rearrange themselves into another word as I stare at the lighter.

BURN.

"It was mine," he whispers, and I realize he's fading by the second. "She had it made for me. I lost everything and when I saw the museum had them, I had to take them back."

"I understand," I lie, tears streaming down my cheeks. "Tommy, what's the secret meaning for butterfly weed?"

He gazes past me to the open door, the tiny orange flowers glowing. He sighs, his body sagging in on itself.

"Butterfly weed? It means *let me go*."

Of course.

I flick the lever with my thumb, but my hands are slick and nothing happens. I wipe my palm across my shirt, leaving streaks of dry flesh behind, and try again.

A beautiful little flame jumps up and smiles at me.

"Fire," Tommy rasps, looking at me through cloudy, pained eyes. "For cleansing."

I hold his gaze and stretch my arm out to the closest wreath, the one holding the grimoire and the cards. The dry locks catch like tinder and the sickly smell of burning hair fills the room. I watch, mesmerized, as flames begin to eat away the gold leaf and ancient parchment, breaking a spell that's been binding him for almost two hundred years. It only takes seconds for them to go up in smoke.

"Go," he mutters, lying down next to the pile of bones he's gathered into a heap, curling himself around them. "Go!"

I don't need to be told twice.

I fight through the rising smoke, toward the door, and pour myself out of the crack and onto the soft, mossy ground outside. Tears are streaming down my face and my arm is starting to hurt now, but I can hear the crackle and pop of a fire catching inside, so I drag myself away from the building, leaning back on a small fence that rings a nearby grave.

"Niamh?" Meghan appears from behind the headstone, Jess and Will holding her up on either side. "Niamh, oh, thank God!" She shrugs them off and limps toward me, wrapping her arms around my waist and sobbing little-girl hiccups.

"Shhhh." I grasp her with my good arm and realize I'm still clutching the lighter. I drop it and hug her the best I can as she apologizes into my midriff over and over again.

"Tommy?" Jess asks. Flames are starting to lick out from the gaps around the domed roof, the fire reflecting in her glasses.

"In there," I say and nod. Heavy footsteps crunch on gravel behind us, and I hear Derek's voice. I sigh in relief as I lean back, hold on to my sister.

And watch the world burn.

EPILOGUE

The museum looks exactly the same as it did when I left it. But it will never feel the same. This is the last time I will ever see this street again.

"Ah, Niamh! What a lovely surprise. I must say, I didn't think I'd see you back here after, ah, everything. Who was to know that young Tommy was a bad sort, eh?"

"Hi to you too, Geoffrey." I grin. I'm going to miss working with him. "Here." I awkwardly hand him Jane's beautiful costume with my good hand. It's been lovingly cleaned and folded by Ruth and is now back in its rightful place. "I had to bring this back to you. Plus, I have to say thank you."

Turns out Geoffrey had *eventually* thought my behavior before I got in the Uber was weird enough to call Derek—his husband. Couple goals right there. Derek told him off for stopping for a hot whiskey first and notified Detective Moran, who Jess had just managed to reach. Derek hotfooted it across the river and still hasn't let it go that he beat the active police officers there, even though he is retired.

Geoffrey's round face flushes behind his neatly trimmed beard as he chuckles. "Oh, nonsense. I only wish I'd realized sooner. I was supposed to be keeping an eye on you," he sputters as I throw myself at him in a hug. "Oh, goodness me, now, that's quite enough—you need to watch that arm, my dear." I grin at him again.

"OK. I'm not going to stay long, I just wanted to give you the dress. Oh, and this." I pull the lighter from the folds of my sling and hold it out to him, flat on my palm.

"Exquisite," he breathes, fetching another pair of glasses from his top pocket and switching them with the pair he's wearing. "It looks remarkably like the one we used to have. Where did you get this?"

"Um . . ." I glance over at the doorway, toward my sister, who is huddled next to my parents. They flew straight over after the police had been in touch about their delinquent children. They weren't happy with us, and they don't even know the whole story. I spoke to Jess and Will the morning after the fire, and we decided that it was probably best to *slightly* tinker with the truth for some people. I don't want to end up in a psychiatric ward somewhere. I think I've made a friend for life in Jess, though; we're already planning her trip to come visit me at home. Not that I've told my parents yet.

My insides tug a little as a bittersweet memory leads me to the best fib I can think of.

"Mud larking," I say, and Geoffrey's eyes light up. "I found it. On the Thames, just near here."

"Marvelous! May I?" He picks it up from my hand and begins to study it. "Early nineteenth century, I think, possible eighteen thirties. Very unusual, though, and certainly handmade, based on a very early German model. See this here?" He points to a monogram, a pair of swooping hearts wearing a crown, decorated with a thistle, and two swirling initials wrapped around one another. "This is a Luckenbooth. It originated in Scotland and shows it was a love token, something probably given to a man by his lover. It was often used as a sign of betrothment, or engagement. I can't quite make out the initials. . . ." He holds the lighter away from him and I fill the silence.

"That's a *J*." I point with my good hand. "And a *T*."

"Oh, yes, good eye!" He smooths a thumb over the initials again. "*J* and *T*. I wonder who they were."

If only he knew.

"Well, thank you, my dear—that's quite lovely to see." He drops it back into my palm. "You did have a license, I take it? To mud lark?"

"Errr, yes?"

He regards me slyly. "Our little secret, then. Well, finders keepers, I suppose. Enjoy it—it's a wonderful little trinket."

"Oh, no." I hold it up to him. "I want to donate it to the museum. Something to remember me by."

"Really?" he blusters, red creeping back into his cheeks.

"Well, that's very kind. We do need to replace some of the stolen objects."

"Really." I drop it into his hand, trying not to feel guilty about the priceless things I destroyed in the mausoleum. I turn to see my mother glancing at her watch. "I'd better go," I say. "Traveling home today."

"Oh, dear. You didn't make the cut with your essay, then?"

"No. But that's all right. Some things just aren't meant to be, I guess." Jasmine was awarded the spot after handing in a stellar essay (that I suspect Will wrote the majority of), not that she needed the scholarship. However, to my delight, she was kicked out of the course when she was caught shoplifting in Harrods. Turns out she has a bad case of kleptomania, which I should have known when I saw her wearing my cardigan. She's welcome to keep that one, though—the rest of my London wardrobe is currently hanging on a rack in Jess's local charity shop. Ben from the creepy theater party was given the scholarship instead, but I don't care anymore. I glance back at my family and my heart swells. I just have more important things to care about right now. "Geoffrey?"

"Mmm?"

"Can I have one last walk around?"

"Of course! You're always welcome, my dear." He reaches out a huge paw and shakes my good arm just a touch too firmly. "It has been a joy to meet and work with you."

"You too, Geoffrey."

I turn to Mom and Daddy and hold a finger at them.

"One minute," I mouth, earning a glare in response, but they don't stop me. I take a deep breath and make a beeline for the parlor, not stopping until I reach the portrait of Jane.

"Thank you," I whisper. She doesn't move, of course, and I feel absurd talking to a painting, but I have no idea what else to do. I mean, I did burn her eternal resting place down.

I start to turn away, when a small golden glint catches my eye. I glance down at her painted hands, rosy and lightly freckled, one placed on top of the other, and there it is. A thin, gold band decorates her wedding ring finger, something I'm sure wasn't there before. I smile sadly and turn away, walking through the museum and toward my family.

I'm going home.

ACKNOWLEDGMENTS

First of all, thank you for buying and reading my book all the way to the end. You are the best. Sorry about the nightmares.

A huge thank-you to my fabulous agent, Stephanie Thwaites, who saw the potential in this weird little book from day one. Your guidance, enthusiasm, and occasional soothing of my writerly neurosis has kept my head above water, and I couldn't ask for a better champion of my writing. A huge thank-you must also go to Anna Davies and Jennifer Kerslake at CBC for making sure we connected and to Isobel Gahan for keeping me organized (and for the gloriously creepy submission boxes).

To Yasmin Morrissey, my UK editor extraordinaire—you "got" this book in a way I could only have dreamed of. I hope we keep trading doggy pics and stories about Galtee cheese for a long time to come. Thank you for taking a chance on me. Massive thanks must also go to Gen Herr for her insightful copy edits and Peter Matthews for his keen eye—and for teaching me that "any more" is actually two words. Thanks to Lauren Fortune for plying me with books and talking all things Point Horror. A massive thank-you to Harriet Dunlea, who organized the most exciting debut launch ever. Prob best we didn't go with the Zoom séance, though.

Super special thanks to my US editor, Ali Romig, for being so enthusiastic about my stories and wanting more of them. To everyone at Delacorte Press and Penguin Random House who have welcomed me with open arms, particularly Beverly Horowitz, Wendy Loggia, and Barbara Marcus. I'm so happy to be a part of the team; thank you for putting your faith in me.

To my mum and dad. Where do I begin? I could not have wished for greater parents. Your love and support have been evident throughout my life and I feel lucky that as an adult, I now class you as two of my best friends. I am so proud of and thankful for you both. Thank you for always letting me follow my dreams and never monitoring what I was reading. This book probably wouldn't exist if you knew what kind of books Stephen King wrote when I was bringing them back from the library aged twelve. I love you both so much— thank you for everything.

Finally, to my best friend and partner in crime, Luke. Whatever I did to deserve you is a mystery to me, but you continue to make me smile every single day. Thank you for encouraging me to write and never letting me give up on anything. Thank you for letting me bring Loli into our lives.

Thank you for traveling the world with me, for putting up with my schemes and my phases, and for looking after me when things get dark. You will always be the light that brings me home, and I pray we have a long and healthy life together. I love you.

READ MORE FROM CYNTHIA MURPHY

CYNTHIA MURPHY

WIN ☐

LOSE ☐

KILL ☐

DIE ☒

"A lethal, high-stakes thriller that gave me whiplash and trust issues."
—NATASHA PRESTON, #1 New York Times bestselling author of The Fear

"Witty, atmospheric, and a little bit evil."
—KATHRYN FOXFIELD, author of Good Girls Die First

TURN THE PAGE FOR A PREVIEW. . . .

1

I DIDN'T MEAN TO KILL THE FIRST ONE.

Honest.

It was just . . . too easy, *I suppose. She was already in the water, and when I plunged my hands in to help her out, I kind of . . . changed my mind.*

Something inside me snapped.

I held Little Miss Perfect's head down and waited for her to stop thrashing around.

It took longer than I thought, and then she just . . . floated there. Limp. Pathetic, really.

"Accidental death," according to the experts. That's nearly right. Like I said, it's not like I set out to do it.

It felt good, though.

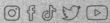